ASTRA FISIC RIDES AGAIN

TWENTY-ONE SHORT STORIES

sister alies thérésé

Cover design: sister alies thérесé & Joseph McCain

ISBN: Softcover 978-1-956998-23-8

Printed in the USA

To order additional copies of this book, contact:
Bookwhip
1-855-339-3589
www.bookwhip.com

TABLE OF CONTENTS

1

ASTRA FISIC AND ROBBIE 'CHESTER' CHAMPION

Robbie Champion was born in Jackson (because his mother was shopping at the mall and…things happen) though he lives on a farm near Chester in Choctaw County and should have been birthed in Nearby City. Anyway, he is a senior at Castle high school where he is finishing up on some certificates in tractor driving, welding, and farm management (accounts and such). He hopes to go on to State in agriculture, but maybe EMCC first. Isn't quite sure. Onenna those things that will be worked out with his parents Bob and Martha. No hurry he thought. He has many outstanding characteristics, or so his sister Maya says. She has always been over-protective of her little (he is barely 5'6") brother. She was convinced that this year is his year. He will excel and be known for something special. Just what no one was quite sure…unless Maya was.

Astra Fisic was getting ready for Castle basketball… one of her favorite seasons over at the high school. She knew several of the boys on the squad and their parents… and *their* parents? Ah, our Astra is getting on. She and Dog were on a walk when they ran into Maya and Astra got the scoop on the pre-season including the great news that

Robbie would finally be moved to the varsity bench, after humiliating years on the JV (or so she hoped). Maya was full of how great Robbie was going to be and how Castle would win their region hands down (and maybe the State championship?) especially because of Robbie. Astra smiled the smile of a grandmother, bid her adieu, walking off with Dog in the other direction. Whew, she thought tipping back her red hat, that girl is either blind or knows something the rest of us do not. The likelihood that boy's shoes will ever contact the court was slim at best and negligible for certain. The bench was his destiny if he got that close.

Robbie came into the kitchen looking for food, sweating after working out shooting hoops in the back. His dad, a one-time player, and avid fan had put up a regulation hoop and every day Robbie was out practicing. See he seldom missed a shot, at home. At school, he seldom hit anything, including the backboard. Here's why. At home, he had perfected a shot no one else was doing. He called it '*the chester'*. He never used it at school figuring the guys would make fun of his two-handed chest pump. When he practiced, he faked a chest pass, and instead as the opponent went to block it, Robbie popped the ball with his *chester* swishing into the hoop. Brilliant. Maya had helped him by guarding him and she pushed him to learn, create, invent something that would work for him, being shorter than most.

The league games would be underway in two weeks as the pre-season workouts were ending. Coach David called Robbie aside and they had a little talk. Didn't look good making the roster so Robbie asked if he could show Coach David something. He took a basketball and from five places outside the key, he *chestered* in five three-point winners. Coach David stood there dumbfounded, stunned, and speechless. Robbie wondered if he might make the team. Coach David said he would tell him tomorrow with the rest of the team.

Astra was into basketball and cleaning her house. Not dusting, the dust would be there for another time, no looking in closets and drawers for things she did not remember were there. If you are a fan of Astra you know from other stories that she traveled, knew lots of people vastly different from one another, and that she was interested in things beyond her professional training as an astronomer. As a result, she had a miniature brass hornless rhino from Thailand, artist trading cards from China, Alabama, and Fresno, and she even had a lasso from the rodeo in Idaho Chief Mike Overcraft gave her. All these treasures, what to do with them now?

She was not having morbid thoughts about dying, she just wanted these riches to end up somewhere others might learn their stories and value them as she had.

Robbie and the rest of the varsity hopefuls gathered around the bench and Coach David gave a little speech about how not everyone can play (only five at a time) and how important it was to put the right guys together for best teamwork and how he needed them all to understand how hard it was to select the eleven out of twenty-five that had tried out. Blah, blah, blah. They all rolled their eyes, especially the guys who knew they'd made it (like the last three years). No worries. But for the seven others, including Robbie, no eyes rolled, only anxious looks on faces as they wanted to make the team even if it meant bench sitting most of the time.

Their parents would be proud. And they might score a girlfriend by being able to say, 'oh you know I'm on the varsity basketball team?' Coach tried to make it easy by reading the list of those who were cut first and sending them to the locker room and home. Robbie was not in that group. Then he listed those who made the first string. Those six guys high-fived each other with arrogance, pleasure and headed off. The second string was then named, and Robbie was left sitting alone on the bench not knowing if he had been cut or saved.

Astra had filled apple boxes with marvelously cool stuff. There is not room here to tell all but she found something she was happy to find. It was the program for Castle High School's Championship win in 1964 (their last one). There was Robbie's g-dad Robert on the front cover. He scored twenty-two points that night and stunned the lofty *Cowboys* of Nearby City by six points. Their faultless season and dream of becoming champions ended. Robert was famous for his hook shot, learned on TV by the sky-hook of Karim. He was not that tall (maybe 6') but was able to shift and move around opponents, turn sideways, and pop that ball high in the air finding its way into the hoop. Game after game he was their high scorer and in the end the MVP of the school, region, and State. That was his year. Then he graduated, was drafted, and went to Vietnam. Things went downhill from there. His son Bob played JV and was happy with that. Now Robbie wanted something for himself. Astra knew just the man to give this cover to and she put on her red hat and drove over to their farm.

No one was home so she returned and decided to have it framed, the paper thinning with age. (She wished she would thin with age!).

There was Robbie's name on the roster, the Varsity roster. The names were alphabetical, rather than by first string and so they felt well a team. Robbie could not believe his eyes. His last talk with Coach was a bit strained. The opening game was Friday night. He had been issued his uniform but wanted to buy new shoes. Bob had agreed to take him shopping at the mall the next day after he finished in the field. To say he was proud, delighted, impressed, would be an understatement. Bob decided he would have the best shoes they could find. Astra had framed the program cover herself as it was just an eight-by-ten (rather poorly) printed sheet, making sure it was as air-free as possible. Would last another generation? She phoned Martha who invited her over and was grateful for the gift. Astra had wrapped it in brown paper and put Robbie's name on it. She had heard he made the Varsity and just wanted to share something from her treasures. They may well have had one themselves, but this was for him. They shared some apple pie and hot custard, sweet T, and a long chat. Astra set off filled with hope for the night's game.

The gym had a sweaty, sticky, humid, pizza and popcorn smell. Folks were excited about the new beginnings, cheerleaders in their new uniforms bounced around with pompoms and their mascot, a *Commodore*, strutting around in his sea-captains uniform. Astra, Nevaeh, Percy, and most of the town gathered to cheer them on. And there was Robbie Champion in his Varsity kit and his Air Jordans, ready to play if called upon. He was not. But he beamed anyway as they won their first game by fourteen points. You might wonder if he ever played, and the answer is yes, mostly when they were far ahead as Coach was not keen on his *cheste*r sure the demonstration had been a fluke. So, Robbie never scored.

Fast forward…the State championships. They were behind, three minutes to play, and their center had fouled out and their point guard was about to. Coach David had few deep resources at that point, and you guessed it he put Robbie in and told him to shoot *chesters* until he turned purple. And he did just that. He threw three in, that is nine points mind you, and as the final buzzer went off the ball in the air struck again and the *Commodores* won (by one). Yes, they did, and for those three minutes of play, Robbie was named MVP! Really.

Is this fiction? Well, ask Astra Fisic or Maya and the town. They were there.

2

ASTRA FISIC AND HIGH SCHOOL SOFTBALL

Over three years ago, Terrilyn came to Astra's house in floods of tears. She was a mere first-year student, and she did not make the softball team. It was a worry, a bummer, a tragedy depending on who you asked. Terrilyn did not play well, run fast, bat well, catch well, pitch, field, or do anything but sit on the bench well. Coach said no, sorry. Her heart broke. Terrilyn's mother played for this team, her g-ma was a coach. It was important. She figured if she had had a sister, *she* would make the team and not her. Demoralizing. Astra did her best to console her and offered to help her as she might. Terrilyn just wanted to cry, whine, and feel sorry for herself. Astra left her to it though she agreed it was a disappointment. The second-year she tried out she did not make the team. Again, she implored Astra for help. Again, Astra tried to turn her eye to badminton, ping-pong, or swimming. No, she was a softball player, from a softball family, and she would make the team. Astra relented. Left her to it.

In her third year, Terrilyn made the JV (they had fewer available players that season) and got to play in one game when they were ahead 13-1. Coach did not figure she could do too much damage. Even her hotshots struck out occasionally. Terrilyn was on a high. She loved her uniform and had a new glove her dad bought. She got to first base and then was forced into a double play. Never mind. She had laid down a successful bunt and running as fast as she might… tie base goes to the runner!

Terrilyn made neither the JV nor Varsity cut for her senior year and as she sat in Astra's front room weeping, yet again, Astra decided to try another tactic. Have you matured through all this anguish Astra wondered aloud with Terrilyn? Mean have you grown up at all from when you were a first-year student? Terrilyn thought so, indeed! Why she was ready to go to community college and play softball if they would have her. Unlikely thought Astra. Anyway. They continued to chat and wondered if Terrilyn had ever watched their team play from the bleachers? Of course, but nothing ever happens out there. Right.

Thee Café Sunday morning for a tall stack and de-café. Astra was still pondering Terrilyn's blockage when Almond, the HS pitcher came in with her mother and sat for breakfast. They did not know one another well, simple tipping of her red hat to the pitcher when at a game. Almond was all-MS first-team, second-team All-American, going to 'Ole Miss to play softball (and study we hope). An extremely attractive young woman indeed. Tall, lanky, long black hair with Asian features. Her mother was Anglo and her father was from Korea. They named her Almond (meaning noble protection). Her family produces almond milk, that delicious substitute for cows milk, goat's milk, anybody's milk. She loved it and grew up taking care of the trees while flowering, as her parents took care of her flowering. That was part of Terrilyn's blockage, Astra thought. Yes, her family is so intent on softball, and not on her. Astra gave a thumb's up for the upcoming Championship game to Almond as she left Thee Café.

Whiplash and Co. had a baseball family. Sparepart had done his bit years ago, even to the extent of getting a cracked wrist that still annoyed him occasionally. Astra drove out to the farm, had a sweet T and a fresh roll with honey, and discussed Terrilyn. Adults do consult one another. Not everybody knows everything. Maybe there was something Astra was missing? Maybe there was something she could do to help. Whiplash in her strident, less than polite sounding and straightforward style simply said to tell the girl to 'get over it' that if in four seasons she did not make the team, it was over! Forget playing in college. Astra smiled at Whiplash, such a friend. She knew she had tenderness in her heart, but often what came out of her mouth sounded harsh and would bring folks to tears. After all these years she had not grown much in that area, and it did not look like she intended to improve any time soon!

Astra took off over to see Beatrice. Percy and Nevaeh were not at home, so a chinwag was in session. Beatrice told Astra all about the quilt club's new project and wanted her in on it. No, not this time. Have other things I need to do. Then Astra proceeded to ask Beatrice numerous questions. Beatrice filled in a couple of missing holes in the Terrilyn family story and that gave Astra an idea. They laughed and looked at pictures of the old quilt club when Angel (of the powdered pink hair) was still living. It was a sorta 'those were the days' feeling that came over both. Need to recruit new people.

The Championship game was in a week, Almond would pitch. Terrilyn was in horrible form. Her grades had slipped, her parents were in a fury, and the weather had been unpleasant, to say the least. A tornado was expected somewhere around gametime, so they sheltered in place in the dugout.

Astra and Terrilyn had gone to the game, got a front-row seat in the bleachers, was ready with her glove, to catch the home run. She had never thought of this before…taking her glove to the game until Astra mentioned it. Now she felt hopeful she might just win something!

Long story shortened: the tornado passed as did the heavy rain forecast to accompany it. It was extremely hot and muggy. It was unpleasant indeed, but they got on with it. Almond pitched a two-hitter, and one of those hits was a homer that Terri Lynn caught. Right there in the bleachers. Now that she wore glasses, she could see so much better. That bright yellow ball just fell into her mitt, and she has it on a stand in her room at home with the following:

Terrilyn caught this homer in the bleachers,
Championship Game, July 2019.
Castle High School 4 vs Modern High School 1
MISSISSIPPI GIRL'S SOFTBALL CHAMPIONS

3

ASTRA FISIC AND MELODIOUS' MIRACLE

Melodious, 64, was not well. We have mentioned this a time or two but this time she felt poorly and puny. Nausea off and on. Weak. Hungry, no appetite. Depressed. Exhausted. The *blues* music strengthened her but this time she had to go to the doctor. She had to go, headset and all. Whiplash said she would go with her. Mel said no. Sarahfinna said she would go with her. Mel said no. Astra said she would go with her, she said maybe. One of Mel's favorite things to do was listen to the blues or jazz and watch a rooted sweet potato grow. Just sitting there with the white roots swimming in the water, the potato secured on the glass by two toothpicks and green shoots crawling out as she watched. Amazing. Watching things live and grow, reproduce, and enrich us. Gifts. Pure gifts of God. She phoned the Clinic. Yes, tomorrow at 9:30am. Do not eat first. Take any medication you must. She had none. The appointment went well. Basic blood draw, vitals, temperature, no covid, weight, all the particulars.

It was the first adult exam Melodious had ever had. She had never been sick or felt poorly. Oh, she had had the odd headache, or been hit by a softball, or during a period felt moldy. But nothing like she was feeling now. It scared her. Astra was not much help, but better than her sisters. They were in a flurry, worried to death. Astra was calm, tucked up under her red hat, and ready to just *be* there.

The nice young lady doctor as she called her (Dr. Honora Steel) explained the tests she wanted to run. No, they could not all be done in one day. Over a few days. Maybe a month. No need to stay in the hospital. Get someone to drive you. The outcomes would indicate what needed to happen next. Melodious accepted a jab for anxiety, as she was sure she was going to die (at any moment). She would go home and sleep for the afternoon. Astra would come back later with some hot lunch.

After dropping Melodious off at the farm, her sisters hovered for a few minutes and then left her to sleep, Astra went to Thee Café for some lunch. Just a small burger and unsweet T. Some of the usual suspects were there but she took a booth to herself. What if Melodious was seriously ill, cancer, or another horrible debilitating disease? What if? It was a horrid thing to think about. Frightening. Her friend is sick. Astra had been through some illness and Sarahfinna, 61, had suffered a few breaks. Whiplash, 67, was healthy or so it seemed. She was just grumpy and frequently cranky. Their brother, Thomas Junior (Sparepart's dad) is fifty-nine.

We mentioned elsewhere that things take time and here is a perfect example. Medical tests seem to take forever, never knowing exactly what they were looking for, as so many illnesses have similar symptoms. Dr. H. was an angel. Melodious and she clicked (thank God) and Mel faithfully accepted the list of things Doc.H. wanted to do to try to bring her back to robust health. She had already done all her vitals, including basic bloods. The results of those blood tests would tell.

Melodious returned the next week for Dr. H. to explain what she had in mind. Doc. H. recommended the following due to the serious Vitamin D deficiency she discovered: bone density test, glucose tolerance as her sugar was on the pre-diabetes spectrum, a mammogram to rule out breast cancer, and finally a colonoscopy to check for polyps or changes in large intestine/rectum. All of this and a couple of smaller tests (including X-Rays)would take at least a month to come together and give them the insight they needed. However, she would prescribe 5,000 IU daily of Vitamin D3 and multiple vitamins, a change in diet that would include salmon, avocados, tuna, black beans, milk or yogurt, egg yolks, and sunshine ten to thirty minutes several times a week. She also prescribed a small dose of anti-anxiety medication to take the edge off. Melodious said she would do it. Astra was impressed with Melodious and her perseverance. She drove her to this appointment and that.

Sarahfinna took her to bone density and Whiplash took her for the colonoscopy after preparing her the night before at home, waiting up as her gut cleared itself thanks to the medicine. Astra accompanied her to the mammogram and by the end of the month, Melodious felt she had had every part of her anatomy checked, rechecked, and if they had not discovered what *it* was…where else would they look?

Folks met at Thee Café on Sunday before Church and were big supports to Melodious who would visit Doc. H. on Monday afternoon. Tall stacks, though Melodious had grits, scrambled eggs, and orange juice. She was trying. Doc. H. had put together what she called a 'care package.' This listed all the test results and the care plan for the next three months. It said her bone density was low but near normal; mammogram clear; colonoscopy clipped one tiny benign polyp, and the glucose tolerance test did not indicate diabetes but indicated care needed.

The serious Vitamin D deficiency seemed to be at the root and that could be improved with supplements, proper diet, rest, less stress, and mounds of sunshine! Already Melodious reported she had seen a reduction in fatigue, mood swings, and muscle aches. She was on the mend, not healed, and she promised to do as Doc. H. suggested. She left the clinic a relieved and grateful person, knowing she had received a miracle (or two). And what was the miracle? She did not consider it just that 99% of the tests were negative. No, the miracle was that she was happy, relaxed, and willing to help herself change, so she might participate in her healing. She listened as Doc. H. stressed that unless something untoward happened, she was not going to die just then. Melodious believed her. That was a miracle. She also became a bit of a cheer leader for folks to get check-ups, jabs, yearly tests, and sunshine. Things fit together. Not everything comes in tablets or injections. Some are just a gift from God, right out of the sky above. That is a miracle indeed.

4

ASTRA FISIC AND THE 4TH OF JULY FIRE

Hot morning. Sultry. Muggy. Mississippi in July. Already in the 90s before 10am. Lots of people suffer from the heat, some more than others. Some hide out most of the summer, A/C in full flow practically freezing rather than going out. Others put it on at night to sleep in comfort. Others open a window, enjoy the breeze, and then use A/C for an hour or two to cool the house down. old different strokes situation. Now, Astra falls into the latter category, though if Dog gets too hot, she puts it on a little longer for him. She parks a small doggie bed under a vent, and he sleeps his heart out.

Thee Café the previous Sunday brought back lots of memories. The 4th of July fire out near French Camp in 2017. Sam Simms, the Volunteer Fire Chief, was there at Thee Café and it caused some around to remember what he and his Volunteers had done to save lives. Seemed years and years ago, seemed yesterday. French Camp is in Choctaw County and has quite a history. One place that can be learned is at their museum on the grounds of French Camp Academy, a boarding high school originally Presbyterian, now more ecumenical. There you find the history of the town, the Academy, the area, the cotton, and sorghum trades, and even rebuilt-from-the–original-cabins and slave shacks from the era and the area. Well worth a first-rate visit. Clothing, cotton balls, and long sacks for at least two hundred pounds of cotton were displayed. Other houses to explore and a working Pottery of goodies. There is a working blacksmith and all these places, including grass cutting, painting, iron-work, and fixing things, are done by the students as part of their chores. The quilters are no exception.

Anyway, Astra was getting side-tracked in her head. Just outside French Camp, about five miles was a large, wandering sort of house, sagging in most places, the porch almost disconnected, maybe built-in 1850 or so. There were also a couple of cabins that had decayed and were folded in on themselves, all surrounded by a split-rail fence, well grayed and worn. No gate. The path up to the front door was overgrown, and the only thing midst of all the weeds and debris was a pink dog rose growing up the side of the house. A couple of times wildlife had found its way into the house, a place to camp for the night. The Deputy Sheriff Sgt. Marvin Bone found two kids who had wandered off hiding there one summer. But beyond that, the old *Flambé House* was exhausted and useless.

July 4th always brought most folks out though. Hot, yes, but the BBQs, and the cold drinks, the hot dogs, chicken, ribs or burgers, and the slaw, beans, salads, desserts, especially the home-made-ice-cream was so welcome. Many cooks fixed their best for that day and non-cooks made them happy by eating everything in sight. Often several families gathered for a celebration. Sometimes it was just one or two with their little grill out back and something on TV inside. Kids ran around. Softball, running in and out of a 'holey hose', dodgeball, or even swimming went well with the day. Perhaps there would be a pop-up thunderstorm. Folks scurried under an awning or into the mudroom for a few minutes while it rained like crazy, and then passed by. If tornadoes or unwelcome low lightening were not on offer, the bit of storm was a welcomed relief. Some churches sponsored dinner on the ground and took take-out plates to known shut-ins. Some considered the 4th the highlight of the summer. Celebrate the Nation, warts, and all, celebrate the family, celebrate the neighbors.

July 4, 2017, had low hanging lightening to a fault, shooting out from the deep grey-black clouds, and would not stop. Lasted a good forty-five minutes, cracking, thundering, spewing down tropical flash flood rain, and spooking people (or their pets like Dog) who hated storms. Electrics went out. The Internet went out. Safety was not guaranteed as the lightning struck everywhere, even cracked into old Mr. Huddleston's phone as he talked and struck him permanently deaf in the right ear! About fifteen minutes into the storm, sirens were wailing especially the fire engines. Something had gone very wrong for someone, somewhere nearby. Indeed, it was the *Flambé House*, literally fired-up!

Chief Simms and his Volunteers were on it and raced along with other Volunteer units from around the County to where the black smoke billowed high above, filling the sky with debris and the House with certain death. Cinders circulated circling the place, shooting off sparks. Chief Simms was giving instructions as the Volunteers gathered. This House would be embers in the not-too-distant future, like within half an hour. The place was like kindling, the trees around had been sparked, all the dry overgrowth singed and fading, the split-rail fence attacked, and someone yelled HELP! No one lived around there, and if they ever did it was many years ago. The closest neighbor was at the French Camp town boundary.

Some deputies and local police arrived on the scene and began to circle the five-acre property. Already the forest was aglow, and Weir Police Sgt. Mae Wander heard the cry. She was sure she had. One person, perhaps two. Chief agreed to go closer to the fire but mentioned that it was so hot he did not think they could get even to the porch. Water was splashing in as many places as possible. Mae was insistent. She drove her cruiser up as close as she could get, having gone around to the back where the screams seemed to come from. What might have been a strong wall at some point in *Flambés* history was now a massive opening, as if someone had driven through it. She crept around, hoping her tires would not burn, and pulled up. There amid flame and smoke, she saw two people and a motorcycle fell on its side in what might have been the kitchen. They were trapped. One fell, smoke inhalation. Likely. Mae radioed Chief and he brought a truck around and doused the fire with a huge stream of rushing water. Both people crouched as there was no place to hide, but one stood quickly as the water passed, gathered the other one up in arms, and beat it out of the fire, jumping out onto the ground. They crashed trying to breathe. Two Volunteers, covered with fireperson's equipment with oxygen hurried in their direction, covered mouths and faces, and quickly assessed the burns. Two others brought wet blankets and towels and quickly carried them off to the awaiting EMT wagon.

Siren screaming, they pulled out of there at rocket-ship speed toward the hospital where the docs were ready for burns. Mae backed up and got outta there as the extremely fire continued to consume *Flambé House*.

Back at Thee Café Chief Simms went to Astra's booth for a sit-down. He could see she was thinking about something serious and when she shared what it was, he showed her the scar on his arm where he had been seriously burned. Most of the Volunteers had, but no one died. Lives were saved that day. The couple, Canadians Bert and Lai See Brown (on their honeymoon) had survived, been badly burned and both suffered lung damage.

Now these four years later they had their first baby and despite the various hardening scars and had several surgeries. They went home to Victoria in British Columbia, after several months in the USA, doing the best they could, grateful for Sgt. Mae and those who saved their lives.

The story as to why they were there was not all that amazing. Just that they were hit by a huge downpour, the wind turned their bike to the side, Bert saw the failing house and did drive into it from the back, hoping for shelter. Then the lightning hit, the fire started, and *fire-up the 4th of July* took on a whole new meaning.

Kudos to the Volunteer fire-people.

Gratitude for all first responders. Bless y'all. Bless yer very sweet sweet hearts.

5

ASTRA FISIC AND THE SPACE CADETS

Not long after Astra Fisic and Frederick Mason-Dixon returned from the North (see the *Underground Railroad* story) a group of young people approached her at '*the dogwood*' hoping she would sponsor their new organization: *SPACE CADETS*. Not unlike Scouts, it was designed to help thirteen to seventeens learn all about the science of space and future space travel. Would they one day be space tourists? Or astronauts? Or pilots, or navigators, astrophysicists, geologists, or rocket scientists? Isaac was the Commander of the unit of twelve young men and women and went to Astra to discuss their project. He had served briefly in the Air National Guard (though the Cadets were not military) and subsequently had gone on to study astrophysics at Caltech. Isaac was a concerned fella. Loved kids and at thirty was ready for marriage. Right now, there was no one special, and so he would devote his time to the Cadets.

The meeting went swimmingly or so Astra reported. She was going to teach them and help them prepare for various badges and promotions. Nevaeh (thirteen) wanted to join. Astra was a little surprised, but Beatrice and Percy were all in. The uniform was simple but smart. Grey polo shirts with insignia and gray pants or skirt, black shoes if possible, and a charcoal beret with insignia. A darker gray sash for awards and badges. They also had a black hoodie with insignia for a jacket. When they formed up, they were a sharp-looking unit and Isaac told them as often as possible. The first class would be at '*the dogwood*' (their local rail-car-repurposed-into-a-science-center) the following Thursday night and Astra (she was only *slightly retired*) would discuss what they wanted to know and design a plan for the next semester. Easy to keep with the school routine that way kids got homework done and their family's lives were not further complicated. Most meetings would be there but field trips to Nearby City, the University, the Air Force Base and the like were on offer. Maybe even down to NASA in Houston or Florida, or over to Huntsville in Alabama.

Sunday morning at Thee Café in the center of town was always a blessing as friends gathered for a tall stack (that's pancakes with syrup, honey, or…) and chat before Church. Astra was full of Cadets and when Melodious, Whiplash, and Sarahfinna arrived she wanted to tell them all about it. However, other people's lives are full of stuff as well and Sarahfinna had shocking news. Their cousin in Georgia was arrested in a protest about voting rights and was in jail. In jail. Yes, again. The sisters were horrified. They were embarrassed, hoping no one in Choctaw County would ever hear about it, tarnishing their reputations. What to do? Astra sat back and with her red hat tipped slightly over her right eye and pondered. What for? Trespassing and then resisting arrest. Not exactly violent crimes. Their cousin, Temperance was wont to do such things since she was a teen and had been arrested or at least fined many times for her various infractions. Now she was sixty they thought she had outgrown all that nonsense. If she were for or against something she could just keep it to herself. Quietly perhaps write your Congress people or send an email but not this. Their cousin, however, told them that if you did not stand up against what was wrong, untrue, or unjust, it would continue. They thought she had a point but did not want to do so. They went to Church and that was a sufficient stand to take; Whiplash a Presbyterian, Melodious a Methodist, and Sarahfinna a Pentecostal. All Christians. That was enough. Astra a Catholic found the social teaching of the Church critical where folks are encouraged to stand up because of what they believe and Who they believe in.

When was Temperance getting out of jail? No one knew. A day or two after court. No matter, they were unsettled and that was enough. Cadets would wait for another conversation. Beatrice, Percy, and Nevaeh showed up, ordered, and sat down in a booth across from Astra. Nevaeh had on her new uniform, and everyone commented on how lovely it looked on her. She was proud and announced she was working on her Constellations Badge. She had already googled mounds of information and was looking forward to learning more from Astra. They ate and left, not a part of the Georgia discussion.

The first meeting with the Space Cadets went well. All twelve of the young people and Isaac were present. Dr. Hannah Edana, the Director of '*the dogwood*' rolled in in her new lime green wheelie, welcomed them to the center, and hoped they would learn lots and then give back in some way. The kids were supported, and only young Ernie (14) was skeptical. His dad was a lawyer and his mom was a social worker. They let him join because he wanted to go to the Academy and become a pilot and then an astronaut, so the USA could rule space. Join the Space Force. That's what he said. The Cadets did not all hold the same political views. Ernie had his. People had a right to their opinions if they did not cause violence or stir hatred. Ernie a pudgy floppy-fat guy (5'6") who was averse to exercise in most forms, except running his mouth, went home after the meeting and told his parents everything. Did he still want to go? Yes, maybe. Sounded like work and he was not prone to stretching himself. His idea of his future and his reality were clearly conflicted.

Earnie's sophomore year at Castle HS was going well, though he was barely a 'C' in most things. He did excel at making sure everyone knew that the USA was best, no matter what, and that he was going to fight for her when he could. Folks frequently shined him on, but he was satisfied he had made his point. His parents thought him a hero already.

At Beatrice's Astra and Alcor (the artist and lover of stars who designed and set in motion the painting on '*the dogwood'*) sat at the kitchen table, eating a yummy Frederick Mason-Dixon apple-crunch casserole (new in his repertoire). That guy could bake. She almost lost to him in the Finals of the *Feastival* a while back. This was his last semester teaching at the Elementary. He would move on to High School. There he would introduce a new culinary program as well as help the band, the basketball team and teach one Junior US History class. He was worried about the 'critical race theory' argument filling the news. Had to clear that up before he did his lesson plans. Not sure where this fits in with his understandings and experience as a black man in the USA. Anyway, Astra and Alcor continued, having designed new booklets for the Cadets, the first one introduced the constellation's configurations in the summer sky and winter sky. They would draw and name them and after further study would then award a Constellation Badge to sew on their sash. Nevaeh could not wait. Ernie on the other hand was not interested in constellations. He was interested in planets (only), especially Mars, and going there. Isaac took one-on-one with him and explained that the planets would get lots of attention but there were basic things one needed to know first. Then things would fall into order. OK? Naw. Not interested. Probably won't come back. His father agreed to insinuate that the constellations were the Zodiac and that the kids would become astrologers, not astronomers. Conspiracy theories agitated Astra. She and Alcor put together six booklets for the next two semesters and the outcome, for those who chose to do them, would be three badges. Constellations, Planets, and Space Travel. Alcor loved being able to do new designing and made worksheets the teens could color or rework on the computer. They could down-load the booklets and work at their speed. No hurry. Want to learn. Ernie did leave the Cadets and made sure everyone knew why. The 'planets are just not that important.'

Temperance did get out of jail and wanted to visit. The sisters had other things to do they said, so now was not a suitable time. Astra looked them in the eye? She is kin, your cousin. What if one of you were in distress? Astra was insistent and the sisters said she could come for a weekend after the 4th of July because if she was here, she might get into a protest while shooting off fireworks or eating hotdogs. They wanted peace. Not policy. Astra reminded them that rarely worked overall. But it was a compromise. Temperance would come on July 7 and tell all.

Astra went over to Thee Café for lunch the next day. The *red-yellow-and-green plate* was on offer, and she loved

Kisha and José's tacos. Compromise is not always the best but usually moves one further along nearer to where they want to go. One cannot always get there from here she mused. Not always.

6

ASTRA FISIC AND RANDOM ACTS OF KINDNESS

Astra Fisic did not live far from Choctaw Lake and loved spending time there. The Lake, surrounded by a variety of trees and a wonderful three-mile walk-around path, provided locals with a hole, a small play area with a red slide for younger ones, and a large camping area for travelers. There were picnic tables, grills, bathrooms, and waste bins. It was watched over by both State and County rangers. Some folks parked their RVs for the summer, others came for a night or two. Right there off Hwy 15 was a place of peace.

Astra had decided to head for the lake the following Tuesday. She had a few things to do before that, including visiting the jail where a friend, Bolo Barney was detained. Bolo had been a boy in one of her classes years ago and had not taken all the 'right' paths. He did not have a particularly dysfunctional family, nor was he handicapped in any way. Bolo was bright and seemed to love life. Then somewhere around seventeen, he got with some fellas down in Jackson who was up to things that gave Bolo a buzz…house break-ins, robbery, and shoplifting. Some of the guys sold drugs. Bolo was not into that. His friends were much more skilled than he, so he often sat in the car awaiting their return. This time he was caught and sentenced to two years. As it was a non-violent crime, he was in the State wing at the local jail where Astra could visit. She tried to go every couple of three weeks if she could.

David, Astra's astronomer friend, came over for lunch. They discussed the recent Chinese space mission and space walk from their space station, the summer sky, and what kind of binoculars to consider as a present for Nevaeh for Christmas. David noticed Astra's picnic basket beginning to fill up and asked where she was off to…Choctaw Lake… tomorrow! She went off into the front room for a minute to get her red hat and came back as David was preparing to leave. He was such a good astronomer. For years he had drawn the moon in his notebook and kept records of temperatures and conditions. Though he had a sweet little house down in Mayville and his back yard rather plain, he had two very cool telescopes that saw most things other scientists could see from their big fancy places.

The jail was not that far from the Lake, so Astra went first to see Bolo. They were able to talk about what he was doing, about his work (the garbage truck), how his family was, and so forth. A good visit. Astra left a few dollars in his canteen and promised to return. He seemed pleased she had taken him on. Sometimes he would get a postcard in the mail wishing him a happy day or something like that with no signature. He was not sure who came from. Maybe Astra?

The day would heat up, so Astra and Dog (on leash) set up their little spot at a shaded site at the Lake. Dog got Fax-biscuits and water. Astra had her picnic basket full of goodies. After they returned from their first walk, she sat in her lounge chair, popped her red hat over her eyes, and went to sleep. Dog did the same, though he had no red hat.

When they awoke it was time to eat so Astra took out the things in her basket…her current novel, tablet, napkins, drink, sandwiches, chips, grapes, and a small piece of cake from *Barney's Bakery* (that would be Bolo's mom's). As she neared the end of the items, she noticed two things she had not put in there: a glorious, perfect, extremely beautiful very orangeriest orange, and some peppermint chocolates. Where could they have come from? She asked Dog who had no opinion. Nothing clicked and they went on their second walk.

Sunday at Mass the priest in his homily highlighted 'random acts of kindness'. The point was to do something for someone without them knowing who dunnit' (not always so easy *not* to be found out!). He talked about the 'happy card' (so indicated on the back) he had found in a magazine at the doctor's office. It said: if you found this, it is yours. He stuck it in his paperback. Another time he was at the drive-thru at Sonic and when he came to the window to pay, he was told the car ahead had paid for him. They were already gone so he could not thank them. Fr. Nick gave other examples and then ended reminding them that random (and not so random) acts of kindness are given every day by God and our neighbors. That, of course, caused Astra to think about the orange and candies.

Astra went into *Barney's Bakery* and purchased twelve cupcakes. Ternice was an excellent artist and they not only tasted yummy, but they were also beautiful. Astra bought a dozen and went off on a mission.

As evening fell Dog wanted out and Astra sat in her recliner and watched TV. NBA play-offs, Wimbledon, MLS, MLB, Corn hole, major league fishing, golf, wrestling, swimming, track and field, strongman X, and if that were not enough sports, poker, and the Olympics would be there soon.

That was only regular TV. She did not have a sport's station on cable. High summer was the time…autumn would bring the World Series (having just survived the College World Series). She went for the WNBA playoffs. And fell asleep with Dog in her chair.

Sunday morning at Thee Café, tall stack with honey from BrandyLee up north, de-café, and a scrambled egg. Folks came in and out and were talking about the strange things happening around town. Like what she wanted to know.

Melodious, Sarahfinna and Whiplash found three cupcakes on their back porch a couple of days ago. No note, carefully covered from flies and they're like. Beatrice, Percy, and Nevaeh reported the same. Three cupcakes. No note. Gorgeous and delicious. Oh my, Astra exclaimed, where did they come from? Who knows? Who knows? Astra tapped her nose and went back to eating her pancakes. Who knows? The nose knows!

7

ASTRA FISIC AND THE GOSPEL SING

Biloxi, Tallahassee, Chattanooga, and Jackson would all have superior entrants into the *2021 GOSPEL SING* in Birmingham in July. It would be hot and muggy, sweaty, and minimal clothing, light-weight concert attire would be worn. Very light-weight choir robes. The concert hall, however, would breathe cool A/C on the audience and give courage to the competitors. This *Gospel Sing* was years old. Astra figured it was from the forties where more shape singing was included. This year (last year's canceled) would bring a surfeit of contestants from all over the country. The choir from Nashville was awesome, some seventy-two choristers (*GospelTriumph*), and one from Los Angeles (*God'sAngels*) had eighty-nine. Some fifty-six entrants from two categories (large cities, country counties) would vie for bragging rights and a trophy this year. The reigning champs for large cities were Nashville, and country counties, Tenderest County, Alabama, the *GospelChimes*. Astra and her friends would be wanting to unseat them.

Astra was not as tone-deaf as Melodious, but she did not sing well, though she carried a tune. Foot tapping was a strength and sometimes she clapped her hands. But she knew folks who did sing, and they were keen to enter the *2021 Gospel Sing*. July was some six months off and after the Christmas concerts and the like, auditions were held for *The GospelGreeters of Choctaw County*. Would Astra audition? Ah, no. But she did volunteer to be a go-fer and was interested in helping choose the music. Done. Kanesha and Flossie from the Pentecostal AME were the directors along with TallBoy Dickens (Presbyterian) and Archie Farms (Southern Baptist) who were organizing the auditions. By January 15 there would be a choir in rehearsals.

Over at Thee Café one Sunday morning in late January before Church, Astra met with Melodious (who was so keen to sing in the choir, though she was not selected, and could not understand why), Sarahfinna, and Whiplash her three dear friends around a table full of tall stacks and hot coffee. This weekly meeting was such a joy and though both happiness and sorrows were shared…they supported one another in their (early) elder age. Chronological age, however, had not weighted heavily on them, they still acted (in some unfortunate ways) like sixteen-year-olds! Sarahfinna is now sixty-one, Melodious sixty-four, and Whiplash is sixty-seven. Astra's age was still undetermined though many thought her over eighty (the new sixty!). Other than some chronic aches and pains, all were 'healthy as horses' a term Whiplash resented. Not no horse. Period. She grizzled. Never mind it is only a saying, Sarahfinna tried to comfort her. Odd what tick's some folks off, just a bit petty! Astra was proud that the auditions had come and gone and now there was a Community Gospel Choir to compete. Melodious, the mopey, had lost her joy. Full of choir-exclusion PTSD. They certainly could not win without her. Oh, my. Her headphones helped. The *blues* were blaring.

TallBoy and Archie had conducted wonderful auditions. Some sixty-nine folks came and forty-eight were selected... twelve in each voice. They figured there were at least four possible soloists and that meant choosing music that would feature both them and the choir. At the first rehearsal, they played a clip of all black Tenderest County *GospelChimes* winning the 2019 Sing. They were magic for sure. Pure sounds, winning sounds, mournful and mocking sounds... sounds that painted the surround with joy and agony, laughter, and woe. Clearly champs. So, Astra's new choir was full of buzz at the end of the tape and many quizzical looks appeared, from men to women, teens to the four children chosen. Most had never competed, only sung in Church or the Castle High School Choir (some years ago). Was this a bust? A waste of time, money, and talent? How embarrassed would they be? Maybe? Just maybe they might win.

Astra was waxing freely about gospel music, singing together, faith in themselves, praying with song, and the like. Most of the churches in Choctaw County had some sort of choir or singers. The smaller ones had a soloist who led the music, down to the tiniest who engaged a member to play a CD for all to sing along with, as they had no organ or piano. Worked well for worship. Would not make the cut for the *Sing*. One incredibly good thing about the selection was that there were old and young, black, white, and Latinx (from several countries as well as born in the USA). There were men and women nicely balanced (no, not the people, the voices) and they were likely to get some great sounds. Now for the music. It was another one of those *Sings* where the choir had to enter a locally composed piece. Often it was the tie breaker. TallBoy and Archie were on it. Flossie wrote like a genius and sang like a star. Her range was deep and high, though not quite a mezzo. Her full gravelly voice projected the agony and pleasures of God in God's liberated people, searching for ways the people might not retreat but go forward, knowing, she sang, knowing that they were held by the Savior...and on...full of longing, full of encouragement.

Flossie and Astra went back a long way to the Quilt Club's third cycle. Flossie had not come before that but by the time the invitation was offered, she was in. The quilts were marvelous. She wanted to learn. Flossie and Astra hit it off and became kidding cousins. White people (and people of each culture) had their sound. (Yes, Elvis could sound 'black'. Was he an exception?) Voices are pitched one way or another or so it seemed to Astra. The goal, of course in this choir, was to get the perfect blend. To show off each strength and talent, and to end up Champions of the *2021 GOSPEL SING*. Some choirs and groups were all black or white, and the Latinx choir from El Paso was stunning. Astra and Co. however, wanted to favor the blend showing how diversity helps create a fuller sound that no one group could produce alone.

Rehearsals plodded along over the next couple of months. TallBoy, Archie, Kanesha, and Flossie wanted to test the waters, so they invited themselves to the County Sunrise Service on Easter.

6am. The football fields. Plenty of time for worship and then off to worship at their churches. Easter Sunday rolled in, and the *GospelGreeters of Choctaw County* arrived, ready to lift the worship and provide sweet joy to the congregation.

Brother Ben was preaching, telling the story of the resurrection of Jesus from a couple of different Gospels. Kanesha had been asked to lead the worship music, not just their choir and she did just that. The sun broke and the music wowed everyone. It was as if their voices rose with the sun, indeed with Jesus, glorifying God and stepping out in a faith that was not always so easy. Many had died, many were still sick, others were in jail, others were homeless over in Nearby City. The lost, the lonely, the 'canceled', perhaps were not there but the congregation prayed for them, inviting them into communities of faith where they might be nurtured and their faith (if they had had one) restored. In the front row were Melodious, Sarahfinna, and Whiplash, singing with all their might. Astra's red hat tilted back as she faced the sun and simply thanked God for everything. That venue of the Easter Service was providential, and the choir learned a lot about themselves. Some members were flat or sharp, some too quiet, others drove their voices above and beyond. Not a blend Kanesha reminded them. Not a blend. A Capella was a challenge. We want a perfect blend and when we hit it you will know. You will know. You will feel it. It will shake yer bones! She smiled, dismissed them home, and went over to Flossie's.

Flossie pulled out the (exceedingly) rough composition she had been working on. Kanesha was thrilled. This will work. Will work. Hear it in my head. Feel it in my bones. *God Leads*, the draft title, would change several times. She had been inspired by Isaiah 60 for the reprise: '*Rise in splendor! Your light has come, the glory of the Lord shines upon you.*' They worked until they had the music for it down, the solo parts defined, and the movements chosen. Yes, movements. A combo of worship and praise music/ dance and routine choir singing. Flossie would finish by the end of May and after teaching the *Greeters* would modify the music just once more. The soloists would be chosen, and they would begin to learn their parts. The reprise was snappy, forceful, tender, and had a punch. God was given glory. That was for sure.

Astra and Nevaeh, a teen *Greeter*, discussed her school plans, her Space Cadet projects, and ate at Thee Café one Wednesday evening before choir practice. They had been friends since she was an infant, brought south by her sister, Percy, who became her caregiver after their mother died in a failed abortion. Nevaeh lived at twenty-five weeks. Now she was nearly fourteen and wanted to begin to think about college and boys and other important things. Astra loved listening to her. What a past, what a joy going forward. It was just nice to share with friends. Burgers gone, fries shared, and a teeny-weenie-small-yummy piece of José's flan. They were watching their weight, or as Sarahfinna would remark, watching it gather around her waist! Never mind, more to love, Astra would say and smile.

June was the all-out month. Rehearsals increased. Booking for hotel, entrance fees, choir robes, costumes, lighting, busses, and the lot finished in June. Fortunately for them, Birmingham was only two hours away by van (give or take). Other choirs flew in, took the train or van, all to arrive for the first day of the *Sing*, July 15. It would last for five days. Rounds would be completed, choirs eliminated, tears would flow, and others would rejoice. There would be a final four in each category. The Grand Final would be on July 20. Small country counties at 4pm and big cities at 7pm. Astra and the *Greeters* intended to be there. Packing was left to TallBoy and Archie and some of their guys. There were four vans. Folks were comfortable, the bathroom onboard and A/C doing nicely. But the gremlins had begun to gather. Not all would go smoothly. When they arrived, a bit raucous and loud, the *Greeters* team approached the registration desk. Not listed? What? We have been in it since January. Folks were bewildered. Astra tightened her red hat upon her head and stridently moved from the back of the room to the desk inquiring as to the problem. It was explained to her by an uncomfortable registration volunteer. There were no papers. Therefore, there were no entrance badges. And most importantly, they were not allowed to perform. Astra wondered if she might not talk to the Master of the *Sing*. Yes, of course, she is right over there. The volunteer beckoned Mrs. Delphi Spinach from Alton, Illinois. Astra was surprised, to say the least. She had never seen her old friend Delphi's name on anything about the *Sing*. Never mind she just hoped Delphi would tap her nose and things would be right. Her woven hair, a little whiter, set off her nut-brown skin. They had met at the *SingingBird B&B* way up north. Today she had on her favorite worn cowboy boots (soft Texas ones with the hand-painted impression of a river winding down from top to bottom). Her deep black eyes met Astra's and they both teared up. Out of Delphi's bag came her red hat, the one Astra had sent as a thank you. They were a pair!

Astra tapped her nose and Delphi got the memo. With them were four choirs whose paperwork had clearly been lost (but saved somewhere on some geek's computer!) and Delphi's staff remedied it immediately. Two were from big cities and the other was a country county (from Georgia). They agreed to meet if *Greeters* were eliminated before they went home…or in the good hope of a future, they would meet after the Grand Final. Done. They parted with a little tap on the nose and exchange hats.

You can believe in gremlins or not, but the rain pounded outside (not quite a tornado) perhaps to reduce the audience. People came anyway. The first round went well. *Greeters* and

GospelChimes moved forward. Winning the fourth round would put them into the Semi's and that was where they had to perform their original song for the first time. If they went through to the Grand Final, they would do so again. The *GospelChimes* had eliminated the *PerfectPeach* from Georgia, and Nashville's *GospelTriumph*, in the big city's category went on to the Grand Final. Our *GospelGreeters* made it to the Grand Final and there eliminated the *Gospelchimes.* And in the front row were over twenty people from Thee Café and Choctaw County cheering them on. Nashville was defeated by *BlestBiloxi.* Mississippi was hot! Delphi presented the trophies and tapped the edge of her nose. Astra got the memo! They would meet for lunch before traveling.

Astra and Co. made it home and marked the 20th of July as a joyful, ecstatic, brilliant, dazzling, glowing, resplendent, and radiant day. The best. Flossie's song, '*Rise, Be Radiant*' won a special prize for original music, and the choir, the only blended one in the whole competition decided to remain together. For next year.

Who knows?

Astra retreated to her hurricane house, crawled into her recliner with Dog (her bi-polar pup), took a deep breath, and snoozed until…

8

ASTRA FISIC AND THE COVID MEMORIAL

Seemed like a lifetime ago since that nasty killer virus Covid hit everyone in the world. Who knew that a pandemic (one hundred years in the making) would kill, maim, injure, destroy, and deconstruct the world's way of life? A lot more people than we thought, a lot more people than any of the rest of us paid any attention to. Famines, tornadoes, cyclones, fires, hurricanes. Fine, yes. All-natural disasters. Fevers, bugs, and viruses were over there, not here. And would it come back in some other form? Astra suspected so. We'd need to learn to live with it.

Astra Fisic had been a hospital visitor since she was a girl. Then they called them 'candy-stripers ' because they wore a pink striped apron over their clothes (and that would be over a skirt and blouse, not jeans and a T.) Now that there was a vaccination, and Astra had had both jabs, she went back to helping at the wound clinic that met weekly near the emergency room. Amazingly, she thought about the various accidents that happen to people while minding their own business! A man from the local thrifty shop was in the other day, his leg mangled from art tables pinning him down to the floor, causing a surgery, cutting away lots of muscle down to the bone. He would be coming weekly until it healed (or he lost his lower leg). Just minding his own business, like opening a door and the five eight-foot tables, not where they should have been, fell and squashed his leg. Aqua therapy would have been nice once healed. Astra felt so sorry for him, but he had good home care and she looked forward to helping him in the weeks to follow.

The buzz around '*the dogwood'* and Thee Café was the planning of a Covid Memorial for the County. Not a church service, but a marker, a remembrance, a monument of some sort, perhaps something life-giving. Many had died or were still ill, long-haulers needed support, all needed to be remembered. Alcor, the artist, Beatrice, Percy and Nevaeh, Raymond and RodX, housepainters, and Sparepart with his Aunt Whiplash were in attendance. They would recruit others in due course. SueSue, the owner, came out to meet and greet as many of them had worked on the Thee Café make-over a few years ago. Now, what were they up to? Dr. Wendell Dexter, MD was the convener, taking the lead to design some sort of an appropriate Memorial. Astra was on the bench ready for her assignment!

Sparepart, you might remember from Little League, had gone on to college and become an engineer, and was working for *Welcome Wellness Placid Pools* near Ridgeland in Jackson. He loved his job creating small, medium, and large pools for backyards, schools, hospitals, and he'd even worked on an Olympic size pool in Atlanta. They worked in fiberglass, vinyl, or concrete. Any shape, any color, waterfalls, Jacuzzis, salt or freshwater, lap lanes, fire features. Name it. Often the customer, especially those on the high end had ideas for renovating their whole property…so they wanted trees, plants, rocks, and diving boards. Water slides figured in as well as lighting for day or night. Some went as far as to include outdoor kitchens, tables, and stools in the water to float up and snack. Nothing was impossible unless the land upon which it was to be built had problems. When asked to be on this committee Sparepart felt gratified, looking to give back. He had been away at college but was now back living in Choctaw County and wanted to help. Dr. Warner would see how he might best contribute.

Thee Café, Sunday morning before church, Astra, Melodious, Sarahfinna, and Whiplash met for tall stacks, scrambled eggs, and very crispy bacon (not good for their tummies but tasty) coffee and chat. Whiplash was full of Sparepart. How he had grown into a man, was so handsome, tanned, and vibrant (smart, clever, creative, thoughtful, kind…yada, yada.). Well, she was proud of him and was proud he was on the Memorial Committee.

Astra was thinking out loud. What kind of a Memorial could honor over 700,000 people just in the USA? Mississippi was never a virus epicenter but enough had died and some from Choctaw County. What would honor them? They all agreed that something life-giving and helped others, rather than just a standing- there thing (no matter how beautiful) in stone-cold concrete would be best. What though? Whiplash had an idea. She would let them know! Whiplash shot out the double doors and disappeared from the parking lot. Astra and the rest continued. Naming a clinic library after them? How about a small research center at the University in Nearby City? Giving money to a developing nation, maybe a County they could twin with? Making sure vaccines got to the poorest here and abroad. Or? Time for church and they would meet with Dr. Warner on Thursday evening for another brainstorming meeting. Astra had had an idea too.

Sparepart was glued to the set. Mississippi State and Vanderbilt both SEC teams were playing in the College World Series in Omaha. He knew it was Thursday night, but he was not going to any meeting. He was a baseball geek. Sparepart would go along with whatever the committee chose, as he was staying right there on his couch, with a light beer, nachos and cheese, a hot dog he'd grilled himself, and whatever else he fancied as the game progressed. He had forgotten he was supposed to pick up Aunt Whiplash and when she phoned in the third inning of the third game, he felt cross. Where was he? Why was he there and not at hers? Etc. He had no good excuse except the truth, and she did not buy it. He could go pick her up and drop her off and hurry home. No. He would phone Astra. He told Aunt Whiplash someone would be by, to please give his apologies, and he would talk with her tomorrow. He hung up. Whiplash was exceedingly grumpy. Astra was on her way.

The meeting was well-attended though Raymond was also a baseball fan and would have liked to see the game live. (Nevaeh as well). RodX loved soccer and there was a Cup or two on the line he enjoyed watching. Soon there would be nearly four weeks of the whole Olympics. Thought it was a bit risky as covid was still in various deviant forms. The Japanese were not all that happy for athletes from the world to gather. But, big bucks, local business, paying for the stadiums and venues, big TV time, and even if you wanted to show any sympathy, these athletes had already been primed over a year ago. They were ready. The Olympic committee continued to call the games 2020…so much money had been spent on adverts and gear.

Dr. Dexter had a full agenda and presented it to the members. He had assembled a power point with slides of various monuments, flags, curiosities, and pools. Right pools. Sparepart at his last meeting with Dexter had suggested a wellness pool and downloaded some pics for the meeting. Dexter was sorry he was not there to explain but Dexter had worked at a hospital with a Wellness Center that included a pool. Melodious said she had suggested they include one when they built the new hospital some years ago. Not enough money she was told. Preventative medicine is a better investment than after care or death. There is money out there, the right folks must be tapped and see that your project is in *their* interest. So many with various heart, arthritis, and other injuries around. Everyone would benefit. After half an hour the decision was made: their Memorial would be a Wellness pool with a Jacuzzi, two lap lanes, and warm fresh water. Various aspects of needed research were divvied out and Whiplash was no longer grumpy. She had also had that same idea over at Thee Café. Sparepart (even in his absence) was appointed chief designer. Astra took Whiplash home and looked forward to crawling into bed with Dog and falling asleep. Whiplash (and her sisters) tended to hold grudges longer than necessary. Hers was clear the next time she met up with Sparepart. Thomas Junior (his father) had always taught him to let things go after they were over. Like Over. No need to relive, repeat, or rehearse things, especially if they were uncomfortable. It did not mean that all was forgotten. It meant that there might have been a good reason, or another point of view to consider, or forgiveness that needed to be given. Then get on with it. Realign the relationship. Say sorry. Or accept the apology. Live free of burden and resentment. This project, now named the *Choctaw County Wellness Memorial Pool*, would take a while. The committee headed by Dr. Dexter and Sparepart spent many months making decisions about construction, design, and how to get the money. Astra was on the design committee but had an idea about the money. They figured they would need about $100,000 for the whole project. That would include a fiberglass pre-engineered in-ground shape, two vinyl-lined 25-yard lap pools, and a Jacuzzi. In the end, the pools would be enclosed with a wonderful clear dome ceiling, so no cover is needed. Yes, pools. There would be a wonderful wader for children. They would also build some dressing/bathrooms with lockers. This was a big wish list but the committee, having met for over a year would be proud to remember their loved ones and all those who passed in the COVID pandemic.

We will have to wait a little longer, though, to see just what happened and how the Memorial was finished. Oh, Sparepart realized he had been rather immature and selfish and apologized to Whiplash and the committee. Whiplash apologized to him for being so cross and holding a grudge. They are huggin' again! (Oh, his MSU team won! National Champs.).

9

ASTRA FISIC AT GREENIE'S LONE PINE PALACE

Down the highway, a piece from Astra's home is the Lone Pine Palace. No not a drinking place, not a dancing place, not even an eating place…no, it is the laundromat. Greenies have been in operation since 1965 when C. Wendel Greene came to town. He and his wife Bonnie, with their two children, Blessing and Bubba (some do name their sons this), started with a small store on the property left him by his g-pa. Things did not go well and C. Wendel needed more money for his family. An opportunity came when an acquaintance sold him land, barren except for one lone pine tree. There he built his laundromat and Bubba Jr. still runs it. When Bubba Jr. took over in 2000, he doubled its size and though several pine trees surround it, he left most of the name intact (substituting Palace as his g-daddy had wash house).

Astra had been volunteering over at '*the dogwood*' for the week, dusting, doing things assigned her by Dr. Edana. Spring cleaning in any household can be a drama. Why dust that has survived the winter is there smiling at you, daring you to move it. Move it you must. So, all the items, books, and treasures were taken out of each glass case, off each shelf, dusted, and carefully put back. Stacks of cataloging on the computer of new items, and she even weeded around some of the '*Ractors 'n Rucks'* in the garden outside. Astra used stacks of old rags for the projects and now at the end of the last day, she bundled them up, put them in the back seat of her car, and rode home. Dog awaited her. She hung her red hat in its spot, made a cuppa de-café, and sat down.

About a week later Astra received a phone call from Edana wanting to know where the *Mississippi Agate* was. Astra said she had no idea and had dusted it like all the other stuff and put it back. What did Edana think? Well, she did not know what to think though she was a little short with Astra, having just a hint of accusing in her voice. Astra felt so bad, she knew she had taken extreme care over that treasure, found by Abigail (see '*the dogwood'* story). Where on earth could it be?

Melodious was coming for lunch and then they were going down to Greenies. Astra had been busy with another project, not attending to the rags wash. Must have been two garbage bags full. Astra made a special lunch for Melodious, now carefully watching what she ate. Whole wheat pita bread, toasted with avocado, tomato, a squeeze of light mayo, followed by honey dew melon, watermelon cubed, and some grapes with sprinkled coconut on top. Yummy! Drink choices included de-café, cold coffee, water, or diet 'dew. They had not been together alone for some weeks as everyone was getting work done around their houses. Sarahfinna had been painting their barn and Whiplash and Sparepart had been moving old furniture out and replacing it with some new lighter-to-move stuff. They were not getting any younger. She was full of how Sparepart and his company were getting to work on the Covid Memorial Pool's layout, hoping that just after Christmas to present it to the Council. Would be something indeed.

It is always good to have a friend to talk things over with, especially if it's something you do not understand. So, Astra shared the tragedy of the missing Mississippi agate with Mel. She looked at her with that quirky look only Mel has and said, so what? What does that have to do with you? Of course, Astra wanted to agree with her but hesitated. She was the last one (she thought) who had been in that section, and she knew she had dusted it and returned it to its stand. Well, what about who came after? You do not know, do you? Astra agreed she did not as it was a full week before Edana phoned her and has not phoned her since. Something to consider. They washed up the few dishes and headed out to the Palace.

After going through the bank's drive-thru and getting enough quarters, they set out down Highway 15 for Greenie's. Mel wore her headset and Astra drove in peace. When they arrived, the place was full of people. Astra did not ever remember it quite that busy, but they had chosen a Saturday mid-morn and maybe that was why? All fifteen washers were full, and the ten large driers were as well. Though they had two big bags they thought all the rags would easily fit into one large washer. They had to wait for half an hour for one to come free. Astra had some errands to run in Nearby City and left Mel in charge of finishing the washing and drying and would pick her up in an hour or so. While Mel was doing her job a friend Karen came in with a bundle of books. She regularly left books, coloring books, crayons, puzzles on one of the folding tables in the corner for kids to use there or take home. Most of the folks using Greenies have no machine in their home so it was a weekly (at least) chore and little kids can be a nuisance, screaming, crying, lying down on the floor, and such. So, Karen, committed to literacy, began putting (as close to new as she could find) books there and every time she returned there were none to be seen. This week she had purchased some from the local thrifty shop and had received donations from neighbors and friends. They chatted for a minute and Karen was off. Mel put all the wash in the dryer and went back to her magazine and headset.

The drying was just winding down when Astra returned, just in time to share the folding and then back to '*the dogwood*'. My, my what a stack. If you did not know what they were you might think of them as a stack of fifties cloth diapers. But no, just rags for dusting, one of Astra's least favorite things to do. As they bagged up the rags and headed for the door, they noticed a tiny child chewing on something. It had a little gleam and Astra bent down and wanted to see. Of course, the child screamed, and then her mother came over and wanted to know what Astra was doing to her child …and... well, Mel told them all to hush, put the headset on the child's head (followed by a huge smile), reached down and pulled the Mississippi agate out of her mouth. Indeed! Yup! Must have fallen out of a rag, though Mel had not seen it. Maybe when transferring from washer to dryer it fell, and the little crumb-cruncher crawled by and saw such a pretty thing and made it her own. They all stood there staring at one another. Astra explained to the mother, Flo (and her child, Flower) what had happened and thanked them for their kindness. Flo apologized for getting a little het' up earlier.

Mel and Astra headed for '*the dogwood*' and Edana who was working. They decided it best to have Mel give her the agate after Astra returned the rags. Might take the edge off as Edana was still flummoxed and cross about its loss. Edana met them at the door and was ready to just take the bag and go when Mel interrupted her flow. No, I have something you want. She held the Mississippi agate glowing in the air as the sunlight streamed through it. What a magnificent piece of God's creation…over centuries to make this one! Edana apologized for ever thinking Astra (or someone else) had stolen it. All is well. Dust already accumulating for the next clean…three months.

10

ASTRA FISIC CELEBRATES JUNETEENTH

Astra Fisic is not always right, sometimes not even close. Folks thought she thought she was the smartest in the room. Not so. She was a learner, a studier. She could identify many times in her life when she made less than correct assessments of people, places, or things. One thing she learned was that usually, it was not appropriate to use one name only for someone as if they belonged to no one. No, folks had people, lots of people usually, and she needed to acknowledge that, starting with herself, Dr. Astra Fairchild Fisic (astronomer), daughter of Dr. Biella (Bellows) Fisic, MD, and Dr. Frank Fisic II (psychologist), after his father Finisterre Frank Fisic (farmer). Astra remembered hearing about a girl sibling born a couple of years before her who died, leaving her an only child. She may have gotten in the habit of only using one name as hers and her peeps were a mouthful! Anyway, there you have it, she thought, as she jotted in her journal. There you have it noted Astra, frequent wearer of a red hat, a slightly retired astronomer.

Frederick Mason-Dixon Godfrey, you remember him from the trip with Astra up to the underground railway? Well, he teaches at the High School (US History) and was meeting Astra at Thee Café for lunch with a surprise. Astra arrived; Burger was there munching away, clearly having forgotten to put in his teeth (not that mac 'n cheese needed them), and over in the corner booth next to the painting of the Mississippi (guitarist 1817) stamp was Frederick and a lovely young woman. Astra recognized her from the NAACP meeting, Darla Danna Deertoe, a feature reporter for Nearby City's newspaper, *The Nearby Newsflash*. She and Frederick were deep into whatever they were talking about and did not stop when Astra approached, having ordered the *red-white-and-blue plate* full of pork chop, greens, yams, and peach cobbler. She treated herself to an iced coffee with vanilla mocha (and a few fries).

Frederick introduced Darla to Astra, and they got on with their discussion. It was at first about the underground railroad. Frederick had told Darla about their trip and the surprise his grandfather had given him, and Darla had written a brilliant story about that for the *Newsflash* when they returned sometime back. That was not to be the whole story. No. There was more. Darla was there to get *more* and it was about the '*southern* underground railroad'. Really? Southern? Right, Fredrick told them, the trip down to Mexico and over that river, the Rio Grande, to freedom.

In another part of the County DS Sgt. Marvin Bone was chasing our Burger Bayles, who had long left Thee Café. Marvin had been a Deputy Sheriff for eighteen years (switched from the police force), right there in Choctaw County, where he was born, raised, went to High School, and was only away from the County long enough to attend the Academy and return. He married Paula Princely, and they had two (nearly) grown kids, twin boys, sixteen, Bracket and Boxer Bone. Burger had put his pedal to the metal and his rocky retro Ranger ran up to nearly one hundred mph. Marvin chased him almost to Mathiston before he pulled over to a halt, screeching and letting dust and gravel fly. Jail time this time. Marvin was neither cheerful nor happy to see Burger, plastic handcuffed him and plopped him onto the backseat of his cruiser. They moseyed down the road, over to the jail. Marvin was not pleased he told him as he booked him, but Burger laughed until his side split. The funniest thing he had ever done. Didn't think the old Ranger could do it! What a kick in the head! Sgt. Bone was not impressed. Yellow jumpsuit to follow.

Astra had returned home, and Dog welcomed her with barks and dancing right in the middle of the kitchen. That usually won a treat, but Astra's mind was on something else. Darla was sweet and talented; Frederick was fabulous and talented…wouldn't they go well together? Ah, no, she heard her inner voice, no. No messing in matchmaking. They were grown and quite capable of discovering each other themselves. Dog insisted. Astra gave him a carrot to chew on.

It was almost Juneteenth (that is June 19) when the final slaves (two and a half years after the Emancipation Proclamation) were freed in Galveston, Tx. Why weren't they freed in 1863 with everyone else? Anyone who did not know could find out at the NAACP fish-fry on Juneteenth to celebrate the naming of the new Federal holiday. Before that, though, you need to know where some of the other slaves went. Darla wrote the story so well. Frederick was proud to have been a part of the work. He'd think up another story to tell her, just so he might be nearby!

So, they went south into Coahuila State in northern Mexico where the villagers then celebrated *Nacimiento de Negros* (birth of the blacks). Since 1852. Even in that small village, people sang the hand-clapped hymns of the slaves on the 'southern' railroad, *capeyuye,* and thanked God for freedom. Many of the escaped slaves inter-married with Seminole Indians and became Black Seminoles so Juneteenth in that neighborhood is Afro-Seminole food and dancing. Darla reported further that the *mascogos*, or descendants of the Black Seminoles, are now reduced to a few hundred out of 1.3million folks in Mexico who self-identify as black.

Folks gathered from their Choctaw NAACP branch and Attala, Winston, and Oktibbeha counties as well. Over one hundred friends and neighbors gathered, take-outs, drive-ups, sit-'n-sweat-together on the parking lot…full of folks. Burger was not there. The 'grumpy' sisters were not there either. Darla was there with Frederick, and they attempted to answer the question: WHY did it take two and a half years to free the slaves in Texas? Darla had made it part of her feature article that had come out just that morning. *Who knows the truth?* is the answer, but three possibilities seem to come up consistently: 1) the person coming to tell them in 1863 was murdered on the way, 2) there was extraordinarily little Union Army presence in Texas so a slave-freeing couldn't have been enforced and, 3) The government wanted the big cotton harvest to go through before letting them know. Though a big slave-holding state Texas had had no Civil War battles but had inherited lots of freed slaves from nearby states on the move who tried to convince Texans that they were free. In any case, June 19, 1865, is marked as *the* day they heard. FREEDOM DAY, Emancipation Day. The end of slavery. A perfect day to be reminded of slavery's horrors. A perfect day to celebrate freedom and the dignity of the human person, who is no longer just Tom, or BigBoy, Mary, Auntie, or owned. Thank God.

11

ASTRA FISIC AND THE SHARP SHOOTERZ

It was Nevaeh's last year in girls' basketball. Her team, the *Sharp Shooterz* were on a roll intending to win it all. They had played Countywide and won, and they had competed with the best in the northern part of the state. Now…

Nevaeh was a tall, elegant young lady at thirteen and looking forward to high school in the autumn. On the court they say she was a deadeye, rarely missed when given the opportunity, and played center for the team. There were eleven *Sharp Shooterz*, and the five starters were warming up at the round-robin tourney held at the beginning of summer. A friendly. Sara Mae just was not herself. Her brother had just been released from a juvenile jail and was harassing her to go with boys she did not want to go with. Usually, she was the best point guard. Now she was slow, and her shots even missed the backboard. Coach put her on the bench and put Trisha in. They lost the game. Coach was not happy nor was the girls. What happened?

Astra Fisic, our friendly slightly retired astronomer with her red hat on was watching the game, cheering for the *Sharp Shooterz*. Astra had promised Beatrice she would give Nevaeh a ride home after the game. They decided to stop at the Dairy Queen and have a soft ice cream dipped in chocolate. Reminded Astra of her tween/teens and she wanted to talk to Nevaeh. Was not like you to only hit two threes and four twos! Sara Mae was a real case. She barely hit the backboard. Trisha was not much better. Whassup?

The ice cream dripped, and the chocolate cracked around the edges of the cone. Delicious. Just hit the spot after such a grueling ballgame. Do not know. Maybe we are only tired. The season is nearing the end and we need rest. Last week at practice Coach (that would be Coach Mary Brownsville-Juarez) showed us the second half of a WNBA game. Those women so strong, careful, swift, bright…played like a team…we are as nothing. She dropped her head and began to cry. Her ice cream continued to melt, and Astra rescued it. Dog was pleased to finish it off.

Sara Mae's brother, Tough, was a naughty piece of work. He was fifteen and thought the world turned on him. He was insolent, a 'wise-guy,' smart mouth, and a thief. He had other characteristics that made him unappealing to most adults especially teachers and he had been shifted out of school when arrested for marijuana possession and sent to the jail school in another county. He spent two semesters there, participated at the most basic level, seemed to learn nothing, and now was back on the street. He had a new game.

Nevaeh hurried to her US History class, having forgotten to turn in her last paper. It was an essay on why Mississippi frequently scored 50th in education (sharing it with Louisiana). She had no idea. She had to study and felt challenged by her junior high. Nevaeh wanted to become a lawyer, so she needed to be sure she had good foundational skills. Her paper was no credit to her. It was sloppy, poorly punctuated, and late. There were three paragraphs and several sentences that did not connect. Her teacher was concerned and phoned Percy. One had to maintain a B-GPA or be benched. Nevaeh had never been so close but was a B now and would bring her grades up when she could. Basketball was on her mind. Her players were on her mind. Tough was on her mind. Sara Mae was on her mind. Everything but final schoolwork before dismissal for summer was on her mind. Neither Percy, her sister who raised her, nor Beatrice who adopted them both, were impressed.

The first game in the summer league, leading to a state championship, was in three days. Nevaeh and her mates were practicing, watching the WNBA for pointers, and listening to their Coach go on and on about this and that…Adults can be so boring she thought. Boring. We do not need this we need rest, relaxation, a pick-me-up. It was as if she had no strength, she loped along with the court as if in SloMo, and blocked no one, kept no one out of the paint, and let others score over her head without an attempt to whack at the ball. She was so glad when the practice was over. Shower. Ride home with SaraMae and Tough.

Tough liked Nevaeh or so he told her. He liked her hair and her beautiful eyes. He liked her curvy figure and her tall (he was just one inch taller) sweet style. Tough loved her smile and it made him feel good. There was nothing he would not do for her, he lied through his teeth. Nothing. Nevaeh had never had a boy say these things to her and was uncomfortable but pleased. It made her think of him when they were apart. Tough had no license but had borrowed a friend's car to pick them up from practice anyway. They headed out to the lake, not for home. Nevaeh thought that an excellent idea and knew that neither Beatrice nor Percy would. Astra and Beatrice met at Thee Café for lunch the following day and had a real chinwag. Beatrice was beside herself and used the opportunity to dump with her bestie. They ate *red-white-and-blue-plate* hamburger steak, mashed potatoes, green beans, a side salad, and a peach cobbler. Who could want for more? Beatrice ate almost nothing, Astra tucked in.

It was the last Assembly of the year, and the tweens were so ready to get out of school. The guest speaker was Sgt. Wynette Lewis, of the Nearby City Police Department. Her specialty was crack cocaine and tween/teen buying, selling, and using. She had a short DVD explaining the cocaine-creepies and the kids laughed but were horrified as well. She challenged them to look around and see if anyone was using any drugs and crack. Sgt. Lewis explained that there had been a big up-take in usage in the rural areas of Mississippi because people thought it was only in the cities, the dealers could get a foot in. She told the story of a fourteen-year-old who began innocently using crack for a pick-me-up and ended after a couple of tries hooked, severely denying it. Her skin had changed color, her eyes dull and lifeless, and big black rings formed under her eyes on her becoming-bony cheeks. She was stealing from her parents, her team, her grandmother, from the stores. Anywhere to get money to get another hit. Wasn't a nice picture, was it? Nevaeh sat frozen to her seat.

Coach was listening carefully as well and when they gathered for practice raised some difficult questions. Who among you is using crack? The girls all denied it. Who is smoking marijuana? They thought her even sillier. They were eleven, twelve, thirteen, not hoods in some ghetto. She stared at Sara Mae who was half asleep, twitching and itching. Coach would phone her parents after practice. Coach called out their captain, Nevaeh, and asked her why she had dropped in her grades, become disrespectful of adults and others, and why she played basketball like a fuzzy sloth? She had nothing to say. Perhaps I will phone Percy again. Nevaeh begged NO! Said she would talk, but in private. Coach ran the practice, reminded them of the tourney beginning the following Friday, and dismissed them home.

Well, you probably know where this is going. Clearly, Tough was dealing, smoking, using, selling, and making crack cocaine with a recipe he learned in juvenile jail. His minders loved his work, having broken into the basketball team. Nevaeh had tried marijuana and liked it. Not using. It scared her. Sara Mae was hooked on crack and would go for some treatment. Sgt. Lewis and DS Sgt. Marvin rounded up Tough and his boys, and their boss (a lucky catch that night).

Nevaeh was benched for the rest of the season and went to summer school to bring her grades up. She also went to a weekly class run by Sgt. Lewis and DS Sgt. Marvin about drug abuse, and issues that might cause one to choose to use. She benefitted she thought and by the end of summer, though her team lost in the Finals, she was back to some of her old 'Nevaeh' self. She was also more mature and able to say no, even to boys who flattered her. Even if boys lied to her. She was better in charge of her life, rather than leaving it to others to decide for her. Clearing drugs out of the high school and junior high school was a big job but the police, sheriffs and school staff, and kids worked at it each day…not so folks could get busted and go to jail. Ah, no. Rather so tweens/ teens would not die like the girl in the DVD.

12

ASTRA FISIC AND THE GARBAGE MEN

SloMo Sanders rolled over in his warm bed not wanting to arise. It was 3:30am. Time to get up. Time to go to work. Needed to be down at the shop by four. Had new trustees to train. They would show up in their green and white big striped pants, green T, a hoodie, gloves, boots if they had them, trainers if not, and anything else to keep warm. It would be a cold day out on the run.

Max Silva drove the big white fully automated truck the new men would be trained on. SloMo, so-called because he moved at a speed that exhausted others just watching him. There were only two when he arrived. The other fella had been moved. An unusual workforce. Used to be the trustees who cleaned the courthouse, the jail, any County building, or office where they were needed. Nice fellas. Bad choices. One was usually assigned to the thrifty shop, another to the library. Astra noted that these days the guys were mostly on the truck. And not everyone could fit in the warm cab. She did wonder how much they were paid and what the State contract said about their prisoners.

It does get cold in Mississippi but there would still be garbage that needed collecting, and maybe even more because folks ate more comfort food? Comfort food came in packages. Chips, *Mrs. Freshley's Pecan Twirls,* those little round 2"/six to a pack for $1.19 that Astra loved. Cokes, Cheetos, Slim-Jims, ice cream containers, cookies, cakes, you get it. Anyway, what else was in the garbage one might wonder? Astra had been thinking about the difference between garbage, trash, rubbish, litter, junk, waste, and refuse. Litter seemed the clearest. It was stuff, anything, not where it should be, in the can. It was on the sidewalk, in the gutter, on the lawn, under the cars…anywhere but in the bin. Garbage was wet. That recalled another word puzzle: bin, garbage can, dumpster, wastebasket, ashcan, rubbish bin, litterbin, or compost bucket. She liked to make good use of proper pronunciations and exact words if she could. Here was the dilemma. What was in trash that was not in the litterbin? Or did refuse or compost go in the dumpster? She pondered. Dog ate his breakfast and Astra watched for the garbage truck.

Astra had been to the County Council more than once about recycling. And time and again she and her allies were told no. There was not enough garbage, there was not enough to recycle, there wasn't a big enough workforce. They would have to build new buildings. Always a different answer, always the same question, why not? She did not like that and in time she would figure a way to get at least a couple of things recycled. The world was going plastic, and Styrofoam ruled the seas. Disgusting, but what could a small town in rural Mississippi do about that? Well, even if it were just a little…it would be worth it. Anyway, folks can make money, create jobs, create a career out of recycling. What might be recycled? Well, plastic, cans, paper, cardboard, glass, and maybe newspaper-type stuff. Some big cities have given each neighbor two and three bins, properly marked, with different days for collection. Astra was on it.

Thee Café lunch, *red-yellow-and-green plate*. Taco salad, guacamole, Pico de Gallo, and hot tortillas (flour or corn). José took her order and she wandered over to a booth where District B's Councilman was sitting. He invited her to sit with him, as he wanted to discuss something. After they finished his business, she asked about recycling. His face blanched. Ted Perkins had promised to do some research for her and had failed, forgotten. Her lunch arrived and he's quickly behind it. They prayed silently and began to eat. By the end of lunch, Astra was satisfied that Ted would do as he promised and get back to her. She lived in his District, and he was up for re-election. Need something? A good time to strike!

Astra and Dog went for a walk in the park. It was still cold, only thirty degrees, and Dog ran around crazy. He loved to slide about on the grass, tumble over, roll over, scratch his back, and then plead with Astra for a treat. His favorite was Fax-biscuits that Astra made. She concocted the recipe some years ago when Fax (that would be Rockwell's pit bull) was a struggling-to-live puppy to build up his strength and now both dogs want nothing else. The cookies come in different shapes full of pumpkin, berries, and a little sweet potato, all mixed in a chicken broth and baked to crispy perfection! Dog got two and inhaled them. A happy little bark and a nip at her wrist said thanx. They headed home to warm up.

The phone rang and it was Nevaeh wanting to come and talk about her new Space Cadet Badge project. She had already completed four badges and was now working on Mars. No not 'on' Mars, but her project was about Mars for her Planet Badge. Beatrice was going into town to the library and would drop her off at Astra's. Astra would get her home. She was invited to stay for dinner. Of course, no question! Most things start small. One person wants to help another and then others want to help and so on. Just look at Children's Hospitals for example. Children with life-threatening diseases and their families, no charge. For anything. That is because one person or a few people had the idea. Astra could look back over the years and see the projects they had done in the County, Thee Café makeover, the railcar-science-center, and so on. Even the Marble Jubilee or the *Feast*ival, all because a few folks had some imagination. Why couldn't they recycle something? No reason she could imagine. Over dinner, she pitched her thoughts to Percy, Alcor, Beatrice, and Nevaeh. The three sisters had been invited. Sorry to disappoint. Melodious into the *blues*, Whiplash out with Sparepart their nephew, and Sarahfinna enjoying a quiet evening at the farm all by herself.

Nevaeh was all in and knew some of her Cadet friends and others from school would want to participate. Why they could do the *Care for the Earth Badge* while they were at it! She took the responsibility to ask around, google some resources, and see what would be feasible in the County. Alcor agreed to design some flyers about garbage, trash, and litter. Astra agreed to talk to the men over at the garbage truck shop. She wanted to hear their stories.

If you want a project to succeed, or at least have an exceptionally good chance, then you need to do good foundational work. Astra knew this from the many projects that failed rather than just the few that were a success. She learned her lesson and tried to pass it along as the point person, where everyone had a part to complete. When that was completed, they would get a place on the Council's agenda, get Ted to present it, and would soon be recycling something. Things take time, not because they 'have to', but because they do. Whether it is political (like re-election), a tornado, or just running out of time behind things more important… things take time. However, they can be raised to important if properly presented. Often people like ideas but not policy. Or something that causes them to have to change something. See if there is recycling, they would have to change the waste bill…just think, printing all those new bills. One tiny piece. They (that is the Council) would have to find a place to take the recycled stuff. Was there a building in Nearby City for such? Who knew? Good research would tell. Who would they sell it to? The conversations with the garbage men were enlightening. She met some nice fellas who had time to think about this issue and many others as they did their time. One man mentioned that he had thought if he could not do some big thing, why bother? So, he tried to rob a big bank. He would have been able to break into an ATM he told her, but no. It is the same with your project…start small and gitter' done! Well, here is how it is shaking down. All the research is not finished though many ideas from the community have been gathered. What could the neighbors do right then before the new bins or bigger projects were launched? What could people commit to right then? Astra points out three (maybe four) things:

1. The Market and three stores would no longer use plastic bags. You would bring your shopping bag to the store, ($1.00) made of recycled plastic also available for purchase.
2. Buy drinks in cans or glass rather than plastic bottles.

3. Thee Café agreed to stop using Styrofoam and to reintroduce stiff paper plates and real cutlery, no longer using the plastic ones. (Few, if any straws).
4. If you have space, even a little, begin a compost pile of wet garbage.

Astra and the committee felt confident that if the County neighbors did just those things, recycling of more difficult or specific things would come easier. Form the habit. Make a start. The Cadets all purchased *Ocean bracelets* made of recycled plastic from the sea. Lessons at every level for the schools would begin in autumn, right from Pre-K about taking care of the earth. Form a new habit. Make a start. Do one thing anyway.

13

ASTRA FISIC AND THE 'TALKING NEWSPAPER'

With screens folks can read any daily/weekly newspaper they want, might cost a few dollars a month but there it is. Astra Fisic, our red-hatted, slightly retired astronomer, reads every newspaper she can find. Out in the MS countryside, there are no dailies. There is an excellent freebie from Nearby City, carrying the latest in both national news and sports. That kept Astra happily reading. Her County has a weekly and she contributes to that on occasion. Astra has become more interested in podcasts of late and audio books. She had decided not only to continue to author her article for the County newspaper each week but to design a podcast (isn't that a bit like aspects of a *talking newspaper*?). Techy challenged to the nth degree, Astra needed help. She went over to Nearby University, where she was taking a class, and went to the communications department. A bright College student who has grown up with all this will surely help her. Professor Diane Muscat sat with Astra and heard her plea. There are always crosscurrents when it comes to media. One says this, another that. Two people witness the same accident and are sure the hat was green, not black; the jeans were torn, no whole; the car was blue, no white. The robber in the *7-11* was tall, no medium; had black hair, no brown; wore a plaid shirt, no checked. The same happens with the way the stories are reported. For example, if you want your friends to vote for you for Class President, you tell them all the good things about you. Your opponent will tell them the rest. It does not mean that those things are 'not true', it simply means that the other wants them to focus on *their* interpretation of the story rather than yours. If one person tells the story, Joe Bloggs was the first to step on the moon; if another tells it Jane Batts was. The truth might be something like they stepped out together, or each had a foot in place and another on the ladder. It can devolve into what one might call *yellow* journalism or take the tiny grain of truth and spin it to fit one point of view. So, the Professor and Astra agreed to find a balance in the podcast, and yes, she thought 'Talking newspaper' was a great name! She would help Astra herself!

Thee Café on a Wednesday night before church was always more raucous than the Sunday morning gatherings. Not sure why. Maybe because folks had had a bit of time to get things done around the house, had a short sabbath type afternoon, and then looked forward to whatever age-appropriate activity might be on for the evening. Astra was not that hungry, but she did want to see Sarahfinna, Whiplash, and Melodious, her friends. She had been so busy all week with her new project she had gone nowhere but her office or NU. Were they going to be interested in her talking newspaper project? Not really. Not because it was her, as she was always producing stuff that they did not understand (or so they complained. Astra figured they did!). No, just because it stretched their brains further than they wanted to go. So, she asked them what they had been up to. Sarahfinna, you might remember, has an acidic stomach but loves fried squirrel, so she had been hunting, shot four to cook on her BBQ grill. Melodious was able to make her favorite okra stew as a neighboring farm grew them by the trillions! And Whiplash loved game-pie, full of 'possum. She cooked up a big batch. Did anyone want to come over and eat? Ah, no thanks. They were all polite. Astra asked if they would be willing to tell their stories in her talking newspaper? Maybe. What did they have to do? They did not much like anything that even smelled a teeny, tiny, weenie, a bit like change.

Professor Diane and Astra worked to get all the parts needed for a podcast in place. Astra borrowed the mics and other equipment to see if it was something she wanted to do. If so, she would buy her own gear. Finally, it was the day she had agreed to record Melodious' story about okra stew. Astra and Professor Diane had it all set up, the background music, the adverts, even an introduction about *Frankly Family Farm* (yes, that's their surname, *Frankly.*)

Melodious was on time and had a large Tupperware container, carefully stored in a re-cycled plastic carrier. Astra encouraged Mel to be comfortable in the chair provided and just to answer the questions asked. Astra went over the basics… what was so great about okra? When did she love eating the stew best? What else went in besides okra? And the like… Mel figured she could do that as she would just be talking to Astra. Professor Diane was in the other room listening with a headset, paying attention to the things of the podcast.

And so, it went. Beautiful. Astra finally learned that Mel's secret ingredient in okra stew was not okra, but ginger. Mel was as happy as a 'possum camped comfortably in Whiplash's cluttered attic. Diane played it for her, and Mel went home, having given Diane the Tupperware container, full of okra stew. She smiled, thanked her, and blessed her heart.

Sarahfinna and Whiplash agreed to do theirs as well and then the three were combined. It was Astra's first talking newspaper a country column about what people still eat (on occasion) and how they prepared it. Some might see it as a cooking column. Others that it was about hunting or gardening. Or sharing with neighbors. Others might see the desire to inform others about rural customs. See what I mean about the spin? Nothing untrue, just a different emphasis.

That was the night Astra discovered a podcast that would change her thinking. Sometimes the truth seems absent or surrounded by lies. Nothing as simple as okra stew. No something about police brutality. A black man named George had been murdered in broad daylight by a white policeman named Derek. Really? Where on earth? Minnesota. Witnesses described what happened on that podcast. The reporter asked questions but mostly let them talk. And the story, because of the bravery of one young teen, was verified by the video she made on her phone. The other podcast next to this one on her screen told a vastly different story. How does one know what to believe? From Astra's point of view when listening to them both, the grain of truth was so tiny in the second one she could not believe that anyone would bother making the talking newspaper at all. But there you have it. *Yellow* journalism carries itself into newer forms of journalism, reaching out to people to get them to believe what they want you to…not necessarily the truth. Be careful. Astra ended her podcast with a quick reference to the Scripture that reminded people, *THE Truth will set you free*! Not what you might try to make the truth.

14

ASTRA FISIC AND THE SCAVENGER HUNT

Be assured that fun was had by all. And the Grand Prize winner was a team of three. The first *Labor Day Scavenger Hunt* was canceled due to Hurricane Katrina (2015), but the 2016 one went without a hitch. Astra fingered the snow globe she had *scavengered* up on Little Mountain off the Natchez Trace. A peace globe full of various colors of glitter rather than snow dancing in the liquid. It brought back sweet memories, especially of her teaming up with Gladys and Homer (remember *Little Fishes & Loaves*?) from Nearby City. They were among the hundred or so people who participated. I Will tell you right now they did not find the final BIG prize, but they had fun looking. The three people (no, not the sisters) who won were folks Astra had not met before. There was no age limit (or residency requirements) for the participants, just a $5 fee, and, other than deducting token funds for over-head, the money went to the Elementary for art and music supplies (regularly purchased by classroom teachers due to an insufficiency of funds). There were two teams of teachers, one from Winston County (just to the south of Choctaw) and Webster (just to the north) along with others. Astra was not exactly sure why so many teachers had entered but she loved meeting them. The hunt lasted for a week and culminated on Labor Day at the baseball field where a huge community picnic was on offer around 4pm. Some folks would still be searching. Had to be found by midnight or it was all over.

Astra had finished feeding Dog (after a little incident that sometimes happens to bi-polar puppies) and set out for Thee Café for lunch with Homer and Gladys. The girls were in school. *The red-white-and-blue plate* featured sweet potato casserole, greens, fried (or baked) chicken, a scoop of mac 'n cheese or cornbread, and sweet T. They ordered and found a booth. Burger was still restricted from Thee Café, had served five days in jail for his last offense, paid a fine, and had to do fifteen hours of community service. He had never done any before. Hard to imagine who would take him on. Maybe the police? Gladys was full of what was going on with Teeny and Tiny, now teens. Teeny was a Senior at Nearby High School and doing very well, looking to go on to Community College. Tiny was a sophomore and struggled, her dyslexia though under control still flummoxed her on occasion and she needed more time to do things. Fortunately, she had a tutor and someone who monitored her during tests and the like. What she loved most was the band. She played a big bass drum. It was only in this last year she had grown tall enough to look over the top of it! Tiny loved their bright silver uniforms with black trimmings and a big feather on their top hats. Tiny felt fabulous, Gladys reported, when playing her drum. Like she was in another world. Homer broke in and reminded them that Teeny was in the choir and loved music as well. Thank you, Homer. Bahahaha, the women laughed. He just needed to be in, not all girl talk! Gladys bragged on him and his job at the school-bus depository. He supervised the trustees and made sure the busses were clean, the air in tires, engines, running, and he even listened in on the engines for hiccups. There were forty-eight busses in their fleet each making two if not more trips daily carrying the kids of Nearby City and County.

Was not long into lunch that the *Labor Day Scavenger Hunt of 2016* came up. Funny Astra said I was just thinking about it this morning. I can remember finding that glitter globe. Gladys and Homer's faces filled with smiles. Homer had been the driver along the various paths that might have led to a prize, indeed the Grand Prize of $300. Various newspapers within the neighboring counties published the maps and clues. Each day provided something new. There was no order just that people could choose what they went hunting for each day.

Some even hunted at night. Up hills, down by creeks and near buildings, houses, cow pastures, horse barns, cotton fields, or parking lots. In the most 'hidden in sight' places and the most remote. Those who hid the prizes for the hunt were thrilled to have written the clues and drawn the maps, as well as hiding the fifteen items and the 16th, the Grand Prize. Somebody would find and keep each one, as Astra had done. Somebody(ies) might win the $300.

Every day the papers reported those who had found something. Rockwell found some baseball cards, Nevaeh found a 1901 Speller, and Whiplash discovered a six-pack of marbles from Mark's shop. By Sunday, all fifteen items were secured, pictures taken, and printed in the Sunday editions. No Grand Prize winner. Barbara Jean, Nancy, and Bethany, the teachers from Winston County found the Grand Prize, just on 6pm, Labor Day. They thought they might be on to something when they read the last clue:

If you were traveling around town and noticed a door to go through after passing the canon---you might find the Grand Prize pinned to something you'd not seen before. Be gentle with the unpinning...it all might fall. Good Luck.

You might remember the Quilt Club? Well anyway, Astra and several others from Choctaw County had worked on a project for some time and finally donated it to the Courthouse where it filled the wall and invitingly welcomed all passers-by to see the State of Mississippi quilted before their eyes. Each block represented something different about the State...bugs, rivers, famous people, etc. Each block was tied to the next with a ribbon and the entire left side featured blocks done in blues to represent the Mississippi River. It was brilliant.

Homer reminded them how Barbara Jean, Nancy, and Bethany tore into the parking lot, double-parked behind DS Marvin's cruiser, and scrambled up to the desk at the picnic waving the Prize envelope. The judges, RodX, Rev. Peterpaul (remember the *Other Brothers*?), and Abigail (who found the Mississippi agate), directed them over and opened the envelope, taking out three crisp $100 bills! Abigail announced the Hunt was completed that these three had won the Grand Prize. Y'all eat up! Many thought the teachers would take $100 each. But no. They gave the money to their school and beamed with delight at having won something for the first time. Gladys said she was always proud that they did that, not that there was anything wrong with keeping the money, but it touched something in her heart. Any opportunity to do something thoughtful for others is an opportunity to take. The outcome far outlasts the few dollars, in this case, with community-building tools. They agreed to meet again soon, maybe in Nearby City when Astra could come to visit. Astra tipped her red hat and scurried home.

15

ASTRA FISIC AND SARAHFINNA'S BIBLE STUDY

It is unlikely you have met Candy and Emmett Martinsmith unless you wandered around with them at the Loveless Café off the Natchez Trace near Nashville a while back. That was where they decided to get married in spring and Emmett gave Candy an emerald turtle engagement ring. It was also the weekend of funeral celebrations for Candy's twin, Clay, who had died. It was a hard weekend and Candy, who along with her fiancé, is deaf, really missed her brother, who had Down syndrome and died from pneumonia. Astra Fisic, the slightly retired astronomer who always wore a red hat, had gone to a conference in Virginia that following July, at Shenandoah Community College, wanting to learn more sign language and communicating with the deaf. There she met Emmett, who was teaching one of the ASL (American Sign Language) short classes. It was hard to believe her good fortune when she discovered the first half of the course was not only the ASL itself but all about the summer sky. Emmett always wanted his ASL lessons to be interesting as well a practical. He loved the stars and found in their silent twinkling a constant companion. He and Candy, his wife of two months, had named their little

Portuguese waterdog, Perseus. Astra Fisic would become an incredibly good friend.

Astra, Melodious, Sarahfinna, and Whiplash were eating breakfast at Thee Café one Sunday morning before church. These women had been doing this for years now. Where else would they want to be? Beatrice, Percy, and Nevaeh would come along shortly, and sharing the week would begin and spill over into raucous laughter and high-level discussions. How many years have we been comin' here? Melodious mused. No one was quite sure. They had known each other for a long time and even shared that quilting class as well as the opening of *the Dogwood Stars Railcar Science Center*. Seemed so many years ago.

Astra Fisic was full of excitement and information, but Sarahfinna took the stage first. She never talked too much but this morning she looked very worried and had an excessively big favor to ask. "Well, girls," she began, "I have the Bible study at my church this morning and I am so nervous. I want to try it out on you so that you might hep' me get it right. OK?"

They all smiled and ate their scrambled eggs and tall stacks, listening intently, nodding, yes, yes, of course.

"Well, it's about, well, it's about, *OH,* I don't know… that's the problem. I just don't know what its about!"

Melodious suggested she might sing a song for them, something familiar the class would love. No way. Not really, she was tone-deaf. Whiplash mentioned the story of Noah as there had been so many hurricanes and bad weather. Sarahfinna looked over to Astra Fisic wondering if she might have an idea.

"Whiplash said she could ask the class what Noah's wife's name was." They all looked at her with curiosity. "Well, what was it?" they inquired.

"Joan of Ark, of course."

Raucous laughter followed and Sarahfinna relaxed a bit.

"Hahaha very funny…I'd like to tell you about my friends Candy and Emmett over in Virginia," said Astra.

"What? No, we need a Bible lesson and quickly. I only have one hour left," Sarahfinna expressed with anxiety.

"Well, if you listen to the story, which you may freely use when I'm done, you just might find that Bible story!"

"OK, OK, go ahead."

Astra finished the story about Emmett and Candy and everyone else wanted to hear more. Sarahfinna, however, was not in the least impressed. She said she found no Bible story and that it had not been one bit of hep'. Now she only had about twenty minutes to get it together and off to church to lead the Bible class.

Folks were still eating and chatting when Bruce came into Thee Café for his breakfast. He ordered and sat down. He looked horrible, like overly tired and worn out. Astra waved at him. He could hardly pick up his hand to wave back. Astra got up and wandered over to his table.

"Whassup, Bruce?" she gently inquired.

He looked up at her with tears in his noticeably big brown eyes and said, like the wrinkles in his brow folded over. "My Portia has died, and I don't know what to do."

"What? Portia, dead? Oh, no!" and Astra stood in shock slowly turning towards her table. She beckoned them over.

"Yup, just this morning, just a little while ago. Why I was in the kitchen making us some coffee. She was sitting in the old big chair watching her *prayerTV* show. I took in the coffee and all I saw was the clicker tilting gently back and forth in her hand, and the preacher saying that we were loved by Jesus. Her glorious sparkling eyes were closed and her head gently resting on the pillow from the Grand Canyon… and she weren't breathing. I was so stunned I jess stood there and then remembered you were supposed to call 911 so I did. They hurried right over and did a whole buncha of stuff. I jess stood there mute and afraid, shaking, and wanting to pee.

The woman EMT came over and gave me some coffee and sat me down while they worked. She tried to calm me, but my heart was pounding so hard I thought it would escape my body and I would follow her right then. The EMT asked me a few questions. I don't remember what I told her, but she was satisfied so they left with my Portia."

Astra walked back over to the booth and told them what had happened, as they still had not moved. They sat flabbergasted. She returned to Bruce's table and sat down with him. "Have you phoned your nephew yet?

"Naw, my cell doesn't work, and Portia didn't have one. Could you hep' me?"

"Yea, of course," Astra loved helping. "Let's see, what is his number?"

"Ugg, I don't know…oh wait, wait." He pulled his wallet out of his jeans pocket. "Here it is."

Astra punched in the number and telephoned Byrum in Hattiesburg.

"Hey," Byrum's answer machine whispered, "Ain't here but will be. Leave me a number and I'll get right back attcha!" The beep beeped and Astra told him to telephone soon as she had some difficult information to pass along. It had to do with his aunt and uncle, his aunt Portia having just passed away.

"Not sure what else I can do until he telephones." She scratched her head and felt his pain in her heart.

The two scrambled eggs arrived with wheat toast and coffee and Bruce played with it, not the least bit hungry, his head still woozy and his heart broken.

"What do you want to do now?" Astra asked, as Melodious and Whiplash finally came their way.

"Don't really know. They took her body away to the morgue and told me to contact a Funeral Home guy as soon as possible. Then we could plan.

"OK," Astra looked over at the sisters. "Do you want us to help with that?"

"Yes, please," Bruce said, as his face fell into his hands, he began to weep freely.

The *PRECIOUS GARDEN Funeral Home and Crematorium* stood on a little hill near the edge of Nearby City. It was the biggest one in town though there were others. Plenty of parking. Plenty of stonework tombstones to choose from. Astra and Bruce went into the creepy quiet and looked for Mr. Amite, the Director. Located, ever so helpful, kind, and thoughtful, with all the right papers. They signed, ordered the cremation, and left knowing they would be back on Saturday for the celebration. Portia was left in particularly capable hands, or so Bruce wanted to think. All he really cared about was whether she went to heaven. Astra asked if there was some reason, he thought she might not have. He said, no, and she encouraged him to think about Portia rocking, sweetly in the arms of Jesus, who always welcomed His newest arrivals Himself. Bruce said that gave him great comfort, but he did not want to go home. He did not want to see or sit in that old big chair. He wanted her to be there. Astra agreed that it would be difficult but when his nephew, Byrum arrived from Hattiesburg he might get some support.

Bruce doubted that.

Byrum arrived dead on (oops) 2pm as he said he would and tramped into the unlocked house like a herd of elephants, thumping in his heavy boots. The noise was deafening, and behind him trailed two dogs, one large and one very tiny, and a string of clothing that had escaped from an old rolling bag torn on the side. Byrum was Valerie's only child; that would be Bruce's sister. She and her now-deceased husband, Brock, had lived in Hattiesburg for many a year and tried to raise this boy (now forty-two) in the house of God and their home. Not as successful as they'd hoped. Byrum was still unmarried though there was a rumor he had fathered a child. He had been sexually delayed due to his 'short stature' and somewhere after thirty-five he had had a child. Byrum had not attempted to find the child, nor was he exactly sure where to look. The mother was not 'short stature' so he probably would never recognize the child anyway. He had not lived with his mother for many years but nearby and unfortunately had one of those southern stereotype singlewides, listing left and going right around which was found every kind of thing one might imagine from garbage to antiques. The roof partially turned up and water dripped from an outside tap, collecting in puddles that manufactured millions of mosquitos. It looked like a dump, but it was his, as he reminded folks. He was lucky the police could not do anything about it as it was his land, and he was not going to change his style for them. No, sir. Byrum had worked over the years at this and that but mostly at that. His favorite work had been on a blueberry farm where he ate and ate those tasty little antioxidants until he swore, he would turn blue himself! He had been in jail a couple of times for petty theft and drunkenness and disorderly after a guy punched him, but nothing big and not for more than a few days. He had taken care of his mother before she went to the nursing home and now, he visited when he felt like it. He was not sure she knew him anyway. Byrum was getting on himself and did not get over to Hattiesburg very often. He was in the process of taking over his mother's old place, where he had been raised. Byrum hated that house, and he was not sure why. He thought he was going to find out but now three years later, he wondered if he ever would.

Byrum sat in the old big chair and waited for Bruce to come home. Three o'clock, then four and finally nearing five he got peckish and went out for something to eat, leaving the dogs, Gomer and Goober (from his fav TV show), to wait till he returned. Then he would feed them. Byrum did not know much about the Sweet Potato Corner Diner, so he just drove his old Honda Civic around and around until he found a burger bar and went in. Byrum was 4'10.5." He was not 'little people' he had to repeat to himself because he was embarrassed. His parents did not manage that very well and he grew up with deep hatred for being insufficient, for being too small even for the roller coaster at sixteen. He would repeat over and over to himself that he was not a dwarf, I am not 'little people,' I'm just short. Well, that is what his dad told him but laughed at him more than once because of his tiny size. Certainly not a 'midget', equivalent to the 'N' word to 'short stature' folks. Anyway, after two burgers and fries, a large limeade, and a small ice cream Sunday (with chocolate sauce) he felt very much better and headed back to his uncle's place. He had not thought about his size for quite a while. The technical term: 'short stature', of course, fit him perfectly but he refused to accept it. Like a white person who denied he was white. Everyone else could see. Byrum had received no childhood treatment for either bone growth or hormones, so he never really knew what he had inherited. He had shortened limbs and torso, and a large forehead. He had been bullied in school and had very few outlets for his anger. He was not ugly, he thought, just strong and short.

In the meantime, Bruce and Astra had concluded their business at the *PRECIOUS GARDEN* and were on their way back to the house. Astra had agreed to stay with him until Byrum arrived. When they arrived at the house Byrum was sitting in a rocker on the screened porch next to Goober and Gomer, who was eating and sloshing water all over the place.

"Unc, unc," he wiggled out of the chair and stood next to Bruce. "Yo, dude, I'm here to hep' you. Whassup?"

Well, Astra had clearly told him of his Aunt Portia's death that morning at the end of the tape. She was shocked to meet Byrum. The top of his head reached the beginning of Bruce's chest, just over the shiny NASCAR belt buckle.

"Good evening Mr. Byrum," she began, "I'm Astra Fisic a friend of your uncle, Bruce. He is so glad you are here to hep' him and to support him in this time of loss. So sorry for your loss too."

"Hey, ma'am," he stretched out his hand. She shook it. "Whaddaya, think he needs?" he asked as if Bruce were invisible.

"Hey, Byrum, thanks for coming over so quickly. Need to go and take a long nap. Can you watch the house and do not let those dogs make a big mess? OK? Get up in a couple of hours and we'll talk," Bruce explained. "Here's the clicker for the TV. Answer any phone calls. OK? Do not wake me until after 7pm." Byrum nodded obediently, paying almost no attention, and went back to the TV. Goober and Gomer were up on the couch in a flash and Bruce could only remember that Portia would have hated that.

Bruce thanked Astra, as he turned to go to the bedroom. She would be by the next morning to see if there was anything she could do.

"Leaving you in Byrum's good hands," she said with some trepidation. "See you tomorrow." She gave him a little hug and left.

Sarahfinna found her Bible story in Matthew's rendition of the beatitudes…and number two was just what she needed! *Blessed are those who mourn, for they will be comforted.* (Mt4:4). Yup, just what she needed and the Bible class at church went very well. She told them all about Portia and Bruce and even a bit about Byrum. Next week at Thee Café she would tell how her lesson ended up and thank them. After all, she revealed, there *are* Bible stories in real life!

16

ASTRA FISIC AND THE SUMMER READING PROGRAM

Back in December Astra and some friends at the library began planning the Summer Reading Program. Yes, there would be one for tots, one for kids, one for tweens and teens, but this one was for adults! No target group but probably those over fifty would be best served. Would be late afternoon say 4pm-6pm, or maybe 3pm-5pm on a Tuesday, and the team would rotate. There would be seven sessions, two in June, four in July, and the final one in August. Astra jotted notes in her notebook, picked up her red hat, and set out for the County library, three miles from her home. *STAY OPEN: KEEP READING* as the sessions were being billed already answered some seniors who were forever asking the question....what am I going to do today? Most seniors who were still driving, relatively healthy, and could do most things for themselves asked less. But those beginning to fall between the cracks (ugh, falling, not good!) needing some help, a ride, hearing aids, glasses, and pills to stay awake, and pills to sleep comfortably, that is who Astra and the team were thinking of. Get them out of their houses, over to the library, and stimulate those brains, still not so full of plaque that they forgot their names!

Andy Winker had moved back to the County about three years ago from Chicago, ah no Detroit, and was a great reader. Up in Detroit he had been a volunteer at his local library, had recorded stories on CD for the visually challenged, and written a bit of this and that. He had also been a volunteer fireman. When he first came back, that is when he and Astra met, she was volunteering, they clicked and have swapped books, ideas, and projects since. Andy was particularly big on his Black and Native American histories as well as fiction. Big a time fiction fan. Would read anything someone put in his hand. Astra loved fiction and of course, astronomy, being a slightly retired astronomer. Andy was in his early fifties, born in Mississippi, and went with family north in 1997. He liked Detroit but preferred small towns and cities to the sprawling big cities. Though cities offered many perks the tiny towns did not, here he did not feel eaten up by constant trauma as in the neighborhood where his family lived in Detroit. He worked for the Federal Post Office for nearly sixteen years, after having been a local postman in a rich, white neighborhood, where people lived behind gates and had dogs. Andy was never comfortable with that route, though he was friendly with the folks along with it, retaining distance where necessary. After a colleague, a postwoman, was killed (for being black they said) he had had enough. His grandfather had an old place on the western side of Choctaw County, and he took up residence.

He was on his own, having separated from his wife of six years twelve years ago. They had no children, though he had taken great responsibility for a handicapped nephew, Arnold. One day he would like to move him down to Mississippi to live with him. Arnold was twenty when Andy left, and he needed 24/7 care. Arnold's mother was not well, his father had passed and there were no siblings. No one wanted him in a home or a hospital. Arnold was a people person and needed Uncle Andy or his mom, Maybelle. Arnold loved music and was an avid radio fan. He listened day and night. Did not matter the channel, though he liked hip-hop, showing his pleasure by rolling his head and pounding his right fist on the chair of his wheelchair. Laughing as only he could.

The first *STAY OPEN: KEEP READING* planning meeting at 1pm went well. Some general ideas were thrown out about transportation, food, what to read, who would read it…who did they need, etc. Astra already looked forward to their next meeting the following week. Then they would do research and planning on their own over Christmas and reconvene in February. Astra felt happy when she returned home to Dog, and he was dancing in the kitchen, awaiting her.

Winter was on and folks had already gravitated to indoor things like board games, puzzles, videogames, chess, ping-pong, TV, movies, arguing, and popcorn. Well not everybody. Astra had received an s-o-s from her friends in Nearby City about some homeless people freezing to death. Well, not exactly. Anyway, she put on her red hat, collected Melodious, and went the twenty-five miles to the shelter where Morcom and Nellie were working. The shelter was packed as an apartment building (fourteen units) had burned to the ground, leaving people who had never been without, without everything. The units totaled up to over seventy people. Not all were there, of course, some had gone to family or friends but for the over forty who were, they needed everything. Morcom and Nellie knew what to do, who to contact, and how to get stuff. It was in the doing. They needed more volunteers. Melodious was on it. Astra phoned Andy. Over the next few days, they all pitched in to collect for the families who ranged from young ones with tiny children to several senior couples and loners.

Not yet convinced as to what caused the fire the latest from the NCFD suggested a gas tank in someone's apartment blew up consuming the rest. The building was incinerated, left to dust and ashes. Most folks could not find one thing that was theirs as they tried to sort through the smoking remains. Andy surveyed the ruins, seeing with his fireman's eye. Made his heart weep. He had seen fire and destruction in and around Detroit and his desire to get infrastructure on the agenda in every form was intensified. Yes, bridges and roads, but also buildings and human beings. He had decided to run for County Council next term. Maybe he could help this plan along in his County?

The final meeting before the break of the *STAY OPEN: KEEP READING* planning committee had come to an end. They had decided on seven topics and given out the assignments for study, reflection, and suggestions for the Feb 21 meeting where they would finalize the program. Cannot go into all the ins and outs but here are the seven categories selected: crime fiction, humor, national parks, MS cotton, MS endangered species, space travel, and crafts. Each week one of these would wow the comers with reading from books, poetry, PowerPoints or short DVDs, music, or leaflets. Anything to create new awareness about the topic, enable folks to get out and enjoy each other and they even added sandwich lunches. Transportation would be finalized but they had worked out something with the school district to use two of the short buses on Tuesdays and anyone wanting/ needing a ride could just call the library. Andy would drive one of the buses. The assignments would be headed up by a team member, but others might participate as well. The opening bell would be on Tuesday of the third week of June, at 10am.

You might think that Astra headed up space travel. She did not. She headed up MS endangered species (particularly loving those gopher tortoises!). Andy headed up crime fiction, Melodious space travel, Sparepart, MS cotton, and so on. It would be a wonderful program they were all convinced. Alcor, yet again, designed a leaflet for the librarians to finish off and disseminate to the towns and County. At the Christmas Choral, there would be a big poster everyone could easily see about the coming of *STAY OPEN: KEEP READING*.

So, stay open, keep reading, the winter is not over yet.

ASTRA FISIC AND NEVAEH'S SWEET FIFTEENTH

Thee Café would be the perfect place for Nevaeh's 15th, but they decided against it, in favor of the Community Center where many more people could gather to celebrate. Food would be catered from Thee Café and many others would bring this or that. The dress would be semi-formal and there would be the Castle High School *Trio* playing and singing for the guests. Nevaeh was over the moon with excitement. She had promised them a short video depicting her 7th birthday, which was a doozie. Beatrice and Percy were the point people on this one and Astra, red hat and all was to help with the invitations. Nevaeh had designed them herself and wanted everyone she knew to be invited. She even put one in the paper to invite all to come. It would be a party to remember. Only three weeks away and Astra had most of the invitations enveloped and stamped with the help of Alcor and Melodious (who was feeling so much better!). Dog slept at their feet or occasionally looked for a Fax-biscuit or another treat for just being Dog. Beatrice, Percy, Cha-Chalita, Swampy, Roz, and the other quilting women came to make the decorations. They would pop! Nevaeh had asked for décor like Louisa Maria had at her Quinceanera

(Chicanx girls @fifteen) had the previous spring. She even wanted a pinata. There would be other surprises and gifts from her friends and family.

SueSue was the most fashionable, so she agreed to shop with Nevaeh for the perfect outfit. They would make a girls-day-out of it down in Jackson.

The late afternoon of the party arrived and in came Beatrice, Percy, and Nevaeh, dressed in a soft flowing pink dress, highlighting her cute figure, her hair done up in ringlets with tiny flowers and bling on hairpins. Percy had given her a necklace belonging to their mother (who died from a failed abortion leaving Percy to raise Nevaeh). The silver locket had a picture of their grandmother inside. Percy placed a picture of their mother, Caftan over it. The outside of the locket was delicately designed, and Nevaeh loved it.

The *Trio* was already at work as guests came in from the heat, cold sweet T and other drinks were available. The tables were cleverly done, full of colors, and elegant black cutlery, napkins, plates, and cups. (No, they are neither Styrofoam nor plastic. They are rented and all will need the dishwasher!). The buffet meal would be on offer in about an hour, so it was time to show the video. Nevaeh made it for her journalism class the previous semester and was proud of the accomplishment. Many partygoers had been at her 7th and remembered the distress and excitement. Nevaeh thanked everyone for coming, Alcor dimmed the lights, and on came the story of:

NEVAEH'S 7th BIRTHDAY

Sunday morning before church at Thee Café. Who was there? Percy and Nevaeh, Melodious and Whiplash,

Beatrice, Alcor, and Astra Fisic, who always wore a red hat, all lined up squeezed into booths and around tables. It was Nevaeh's seventh birthday, and they were celebrating in style. Tall stacks all around, with blueberry syrup and a little bit of crispy bacon. Her other birthday parties had been at home with Beatrice and Percy and their friends. This year would be different as she was having it at her favorite place. Nevaeh was a grown girl now, at least according to her, in the First Grade and loved school. Beatrice and Percy had another table covered with presents. Would Sarahfinna ever get there with the cake and ice cream? Thee Café had plenty of seats and plenty of regulars. It also had folks who stopped in for a snack or the bathroom. Other times it had delivery persons, big trucks, and cars filling up with gas.

Nevaeh watched everybody, watched for Sarahfinna. She was also watching for her three friends Deal and Marty, twins, and Aaron their cousin. They all went to school together and Nevaeh frequently played over at their farm. Marty was the only boy and a bit excitable. When they arrived, Nevaeh ran over to welcome them sitting Deal near her and Marty far away. He was not best pleased. Astra seeing his discomfort decided to take him under her wing.

Astra began a little game with him when the five-year-old looked up at her as if she were nuts or something, pulled away with such strength he fell to the floor and began to act as if he were damaged for life. Screams bellowed all over Thee Café and into the parking lot, folks looked around not believing what they saw: Astra Fisic had thrown a child down on the ground! What? Not likely. Marty was a big boy and extraordinarily strong. Astra was beginning to get a bit puny. Melodious pulled off her headset, jumped up, and rescued the boy, glaring at Astra. She had *not seen* what happened...only the apparent outcome. Astra looked around at accusing looks, adjusted her red hat, and sat the boy down in his chair, and told him not to move. His mother would return shortly, and he could discuss it with her. His twin, Deal, had seen the whole thing, looked at Astra with compassion, walked over, and thumped Marty on the top of his head, telling him he knew better. All he said was sorry, Deal, sorry. He looked over at Astra, said nothing, and made no attempt to apologize.

Still no Sarahfinna. The party was almost over, breakfast went and the adults began to weary of the children. Marty was still annoying, and Deal tried to keep him in check. Willow arrived after difficult Under-8 soccer practice. What things were hidden in those amazing presents? Nevaeh wanted to know when she could open them. Beatrice suggested they wait just a little longer for Sarahfinna. Moans and groans from kids and parents. Let her open them now. We can have cake and ice cream later. Unanimous.

Nevaeh went over to the table near Beatrice. The first gift from Aaron. Nevaeh tore open the bag and inside was a beautiful doll from Sweden, long blonde curls, and a wonderful Swedish dress. Aaron wanted to know immediately if she liked it. Yes! Nevaeh named her Olivia and thanked Aaron. She opened more presents and the things within were magical. Willow brought a book about soccer with fabulous pics of the Women's Soccer Olympic Team Bronze Medal. Games, coloring books, crayons, and books to read. Nevaeh was so happy and thankful. What a party! The last prezzie, a big one, was from Beatrice and Percy. Could she guess what it was? Well, not for sure but when opened out bounced the coolest yellow fluorescent soccer ball. On it was a big Bronze Medal just like the Women's Olympic Team. Like it would glow in the dark. She jumped up into Percy's arms, repeating *suster, my suster my bestus suster*!

Still no Sarahfinna. Finally Melodious phoned her from the parking lot. They could see her arguing and shouting and then Mel came back in and went over to Astra. They excused themselves, said they would be right back, left in a rush, squealing out of the lot.

They call her Wee-wee, Deal and Marty's mom and she was in trouble. You probably won't believe this, but she got her foot stuck in a bucket. Yup! She had crawled up on the counter in the kitchen after deciding to mop the floor. She retrieved what she wanted from the tallest shelf and slid toward the floor, the right foot ending up in the mop bucket! No worries, easy enough to get out. She has large feet, touching both sides of the bucket, and so she tried to slip out of her high-tops. Nope. Finally, Wee-wee made sure the soapy water was drained and went out into her front garden and sitting in the grass turned her foot right and left. She stomped and clunked, tripped, and made a lot of noise and her neighbor came out and tried to slip it off. Nope. They looked at each other and burst out laughing. It was not hurting but here was a grown woman hopping around with her foot stuck in a bright turquoise bucket.

Melodious did not drive like a mad woman, but close. That was when everything was OK. She was trying to be careful, but she was in a hurry. Astra tried not to nag but Melodious' speeding unnerved her. It still took over twenty minutes to reach *RED'S VALUE Market* where they knew Sarahfinna had gone. They parked and wondered what part of the store to begin the search. Know, Melodious shrieked, I know...*cummmmon*. Astra followed at Melodious' heels, and they headed for the food department. Mel reached the walk-in freezer and tried to open it. Locked. She and Astra turned frantically shouting for a manager or someone who had a key to the walk-in. Finally, they connected with Will the manager, who shot off to his office, looking for the key. He took a long time to return. Will found a key and waddled over, murmured oh my, oh my, nothing like this has ever happened before…Astra and Mel were next to the door, pounding on it, yelling at it. They heard no sound and eventually moved off as Will tried the key. Would you believe it? Wrong key. He returned to the other side of the store, to his office, and searched for the key. Mel and Astra stood still, staring at one another, both feeling quite grumpy.

Wee-wee was on her way to collect the twins and niece from the b-day party. She was a little shaken. Her neighbor had a friend visiting who had a power knife in his truck and cut that bucket right off. No pain, some strain, just gain. She was a free woman and rushed back into her house and brought out a fresh (from her oven that morning) pecan pie, saying bless your hearts several times.

Will finally found the key and they opened the heavy freezer door. There stood Sarahfinna and Rockwell nearly frozen to the bone holding the ice-cream-cake for Nevaeh. Astra and Mel pushed into the freezer, Mr. Will held the door. Mel saw their blue faces and pulled them out onto the store floor. Will phoned 911 and the EMTs were on their way.

Wee-wee arrived at Thee Café, went in, greeted her kids and the others. She wanted to tell them all about her predicament but decided to wait. Clearly, something else was afoot. Where were Astra, Mel, Sarahfinna, and Rockwell? No one was quite sure, but they said they would be right back. Nevaeh looked around at her friends and family, her presents, and the remnants of an awesome breakfast. How could she be so lucky to have such a great big *suster* and Ms. Beatrice? She still had to wonder why there was no birthday cake but even without it, the day had been so special.

The EMTs arrived and rushed Rockwell and Sarahfinna to the hospital ER. They wrapped them in blankets that looked like tinfoil. Astra and Mel followed the ambulance after Mr. Will apologized for a hundred million and thousands of times until he was hoarse. Astra said she'd be back the next day to file her complaint.

Please be there.

Astra phoned Beatrice to say she and Mel were on their way but that folks outta just go home. The whole story would be revealed next Sunday at Thee Café before church where they always shared their stories. All Nevaeh's stuff went into the SUV, and they headed home, still wondering why there was no birthday cake and just where Mr. Rockwell and Ms. Sarahfinna ended up! Stay tuned. (**The video ended).**

Raucous applause.

Food was available, music blared, folks danced and Nevaeh just blushed and thanked people. Those who featured in the film were present and laughed, and some were still embarrassed, like Mr. Will. This time he provided all the ice cream and cake they could eat. Whadda 15th party!

18

ASTRA FISIC AND THE 19th FLOAT

Somewhere between December fifth and eighth most towns in Choctaw County have a Christmas Parade. Usually, the first sighting of Santa, showing off new rescue vehicles, the High School band, and various floats, not more than twenty, some small and some quite large, usually from the churches or an organization. Thee Café was bustling, full of folks. The weather had turned cooler and getting on for winter. Buckets of hot coffee and cocoa around and little kids could talk about nothing but Santa and the parade. This year's theme was *NEIGHBORS HELPING NEIGHBORS*, an easy one for each organization, band, school, or church to create a float. The mayor had asked Astra to be one of the judges. She agreed. There would be eighteen floats or performers. It would be one of the biggest ever.

Long into the night Nevaeh and the Space Cadets worked on their float. They were #9 in the parade, behind the High School band. Melodious and the Methodists were also hard at work as were the First National Bank and Thee Café who would enter for the first time. SueSue had decided to do a float showing how the make-over happened and how Jesus' birthday was a make-over for our lives. Sounded like quite a big job! First Baptist Church won an award almost every year Astra could remember. This year would be no exception.

Melodious did not have a miraculous recovery exactly but now months after discovering her Vitamin D deficiency she was feeling so much better. She had the energy to spend and was working on the Methodist's float. Whiplash was helping the cadets and Sarahfinna was at work with the quilters club. They decided to have a float this year for the first time. During the year they completed a memorial quilt for all who had died or been infected by covid. Now it was finished, and the parade would be a perfect way to display it for all to see. Angel (of the pink-dusted hair) had a pickup, and they could get in the bay with the quilt flying high. Some people were not working on anything.

Some people were grumpy and hated Christmas. One sort was Burger, having served his time for such disrespectful behavior and done community service around the police building. He picked up garbage, weeded their gardens, and was a general go-fer for fifteen hours. Now he was 'off paper" and free to do as he liked. Or so he thought.

The weather was always a consideration, but the meteorologists swore blind it would be a beautiful, crisp night. The doors were open on the fire station for hot chili and cocoa and folks bought them out…so they went to the market and bought pounds of hot dogs and cooked them! They, too, disappeared with speed.

The night of the parade, December 7, Astra put on her red hat and went down to Main St. to the viewing stand. She could hear the bands warming up, the Girl Scouts choir practicing, the Pre-K *Newborn Jesus* scene getting settled on the back of a trailer pulled by a dad's tractor, and the whizzing, squeaking, and whirring of the mic by the announcer, the

MC, Rev. Peterpaul. The Grand Marshalls were Doris and Henry Flex celebrating a 75th wedding anniversary! Astra and the four other judges had their briefing, and all was ready to go. Rev. Peterpaul asked the Lord to be with each participant and viewer by bringing the joy of helping one another into own and County. He prayed the Christmas blessing would take root in each home. A resounding *Amen* was heard up and down the three blocks of the parade route. After the horn sounded from the fire engine, and the town banner, with majorettes, was set to take off, Burger screeched up on a motorbike and spun around in the road, almost falling off. He was laughing at the top of his lungs and folks were pulling their kids close, moving up onto the sidewalk. What is that nutcase doing now? Sgt. Marvin was way down the parade line with the Deputy's Marching Unit when the cry came from the stands. Burger had slid the bike sideways across the street, losing control, knocking over a mother and child. He let go of the bike and it spun quietly into the middle of the street. Burger did not move. Officer Flex (the grand marshals were his g-parents) was directing traffic near the incident and ran over to Charlene and her two-year-old Wanda. He immediately called 911…one ambulance was in the parade line, hurried out, and came to a standstill. One EMT went to Burger the other to Charlene and Wanda. All three bundled up into the ambulance and with siren blaring, went to the ER. Burger did not make it. Charlene and Wanda were slightly injured and scared. Things happen. Some things do not need to happen or so it seems. After discussion, the managers decided to continue with the parade.

The town sign and majorettes set off, the Nearby City College band followed, and then one float after another. The cadets looked very sharp and featured taking care of the earth as a helping skill. Castle HS Band was number eight and the quilting club was number fourteen. Santa would appear high up on the ladder of the new fire engine, tossing sweets and tiny toys out to the crowd, on the eighteenth float, the last.

Right behind Santa was the 19th float. It was magnificent, flowing in colors, flags, streamers, music, and people in costumes doing things for others. There was no name on the float and the fact that it was enclosed in a cloud, wispy and white, or was it fog, or what was it? Almost looked like white cotton candy. One thing, it was exceedingly long. There was a wonderful aroma that poured out, something like peppermint and chocolate.

Most had paid no attention to the numbering and assumed it was the last float, but the judges and MC knew differently. It was not supposed to be there. No one seemed to be driving it, though it moved at the same pace as the rest of the parade. Rev. Peterpaul, Astra, and the other judges could only shrug shoulders and wonder. As it passed by the judge's table and turned to leave the route Astra noticed a big '75' on the back. As it turned left, the others had gone right, it evaporated, disappeared, faded, dissolved, was vaporized, or whisked off, and vanished, or was never there…?

Every year thereafter folks watch for the 'ghost float #19.' Ask Astra. She was there.

19

ASTRA FISIC, STORYTELLER

As we know, Astra loves to tell stories. Even more than that, she loves storytellers and has friends in and outside Choctaw County who do just that. In fact, Astra has storytelling friends all over, even in Minnesota and South Africa! Yes. True. She was over at the Elementary one day reading to the second grade and a child asked her if she knew any stories that weren't *just in books, cauz' I don't read gud yet*? She told her she did and proceeded to tell them about an eighteen-inch totem pole a Lummi (Native American Indian) man out in Washington carved for her as she watched. Cherlynn's eyes widened as she listened. She heard the colors, smelled the incense, saw the carving knife, and counted the wrinkles on Bronc Littlecreek's face as he worked. Cherlynn leaped into the story. Why she could even smell the seagull poop on the beach where he whittled. When Astra finished, there was no detail Cherlynn, and her young friends could not repeat. They had two stories to tell, one about Astra and the other about Bronc and the totem pole. Seems good things often multiply!

Sunday morning over at Thee Café was no exception. The usual suspects were present or coming and each one would have a story to tell. Beatrice, Percy, and Nevaeh were away at a quilting conference in Branson. They would have new stories to share when they returned. Sarahfinna was thrilled that her Bible Study went well, Melodious finally reconciled with the choir directors, and Whiplash brought a sad story (well, she thought it sad) about a friend of hers in Montana. Seems there was a fracas around an old pipeline or other and her friend, Carl was arrested. Many people wanted the pipeline and many who did not, especially the Native Americans because it crossed their sacred burial grounds. The tribe has friends, like Carl, who protested with them. So, they sat down in front of a line of backhoes and would not move until the police had to carry them off for booking and two nights in jail. The court fined them and told them to stay away from the site. They went back the very next morning. Whiplash huffed and puffed not sure if a) the story was true or b) he was so stupid to get arrested or c) that he had a point, along with his friends. She was not a protestor, she was a 'do things quietly' person, minding yer own business, not rocking the boat or anything else.

You might remember Mark and Marcie (of the *Marble Jubilee*)? They were at The Café that morning, over from Alabama with their boy, Hank, three, and their six-month-old-girl, BettyJean. She was precious. Mark's heart was stolen big time by Marcie, and he thought he had no more to lose. He was wrong. This little girl snatched what he did not even know he had! She had his big blue eyes and Marcie's dimples. Coal-black ringlets and curls were already forming on a pretty but still bald head. Hank had been a cute infant as well and now as a toddler, his brown hair fell here and there with a cowlick on top, freckles across his face, and a vocabulary that allowed him to tell a tale or two! BettyJean cooed, gurgled, and laughed from tickles, attention from Hank, and sweet kisses. As their breakfast arrived, tall stacks, scrambled eggs, avocado slices, and coffee, they wanted to tell everyone about their exciting news. Hank ate grits with his pancake and some milk. Folks wanted to hear.

You might remember Mark and Marcie make marbles and other glass products... features like windows and animals, and even jewelry. Now they are going to expand and venture into a new project. Open a pottery. Mark went on to tell that they had hired two potters, Chuck and Emily, and they are going to begin on the first of the month. Folks clapped. Mark reached down to the bag on the floor and pulled out a beautiful peace bird (8"x6") made of clay inset with glass. It was gorgeous. The bird hung from a thin wire and would turn, and fly suspended in the air. Bright blue and turquoise glass filled the strong clay sections. An opal for an eye and a green glass branch through its mouth set it off. Emily had created it and had come to *HandBlown Glass Designs* from an African American art studio in Chicago. Chuck was a local Alabama man who had been a potter for years and wanted to expand himself. They seemed a fit. Ready to roll. As he finished their story, BettyJean edged closer to grumbling and looked as if a nap was in order. They would soon head out for home. Astra purchased the bird, a gift for '*the dogwood.*'

Astra reviewed her second-grade visit and went over to the High School the following week to their journalism class, one activity being the school newspaper (*The Castle High School Trumpet*). They wanted to interview her, to hear her story. Melodious thought that was a clever idea because Astra knew thousands of great stories. (Nothing like having a fan club!).

Tuesday morning, the second period, journalism arrived and Astra, with her red hat in tow, wandered around the High School for a few minutes before going toward the classroom. There had been extensive work over the last two years to bring the school to a better standard, infrastructure improvement if you will. There were now reinforcements in the foundations, new classrooms, a new hall with lockers, a metal roof (better in tornados), and bright posters of encouragement. The cafeteria was upgraded including the menu for lunch and the bathrooms freshened up. Student art filled the breezeway and the cafeteria. The gyms and the band room had been overhauled the year before and students and staff took immense pride in them. There was a little more litter around than she would have liked, and the noise level went from silence to 1,000 when the bell rang for a class change! She tried to get out of the way of students rushing out of the classroom she was passing. No luck. She was toppled by two beefy guys, football players, or farmers (who just kept going). Her red hat fell to the ground and suffered as at least three students crunched and crushed it before Astra could rescue it, fearful that while reaching for it her hand would be stomped upon. Her folder with notes for the interview went flying high above all heads and landed on students fleeing the classrooms, headed for the student store for a snack. From behind she heard an *are you ok*? from a distant person with a familiar voice who reached down and rescued her. It was Mr. Frederick Mason-Dixon Godfrey, the US History teacher, and her traveling companion. She shook but felt safe as he took her back to the teacher's room and sat her down for a coffee. What, he wanted to know? What in the world happened? She related the story and realized she was going to be late for journalism. Frederick would escort her, and Mrs. Jenny Blacks would welcome her.

The Trumpet was not a prize-winning high school paper. If an award were to be given it might be 'for improvement.' Mrs. Blacks had been an English major at 'Ole Miss and came to teaching by the bye. She loved to write and had self-published books of poetry and one novella. Neither went far but she had risen to the challenge to do them. Frederick had quietly explained in quick detail what had happened in the recess and Mrs. Blacks made sure Astra had a safe place to sit. Around the round table were eleven students and Mrs. Blacks. One student, a beefy guy, could not look Astra in the eye. His head sunk toward the '0' on his bright red jersey and stayed that way for most of the class. Another beefy student brought in a message to Mrs. Blacks from the office, and he quickly dropped his glance and moved with haste out of the classroom. The interview went well. Astra answered all their questions and looked forward to previewing the article before they printed it. Did she want to tell them anything else, or tell them a story?

Yes. And Astra proceeded to tell the story about wandering around the school and the recess rumble, the beefy guy, Donald, turned redder and redder, outdoing his red jersey, as she continued. He said nothing. Mrs. Blacks said nothing. Astra continued. What would have been the better thing to do, she questioned? Help the old lady up? She thought so.

Not rush out of classrooms paying no attention to anyone but yourself? She thought so. Recognize the rumble as selfishness, self-centeredness? She reckoned that would be a good lesson. She explained that stories (fiction or non) helped the truth to surface and often a lesson to be learned.

Mrs. Blacks escorted Astra out to the parking lot. Behind them was Donald who grunted as he waddled at slow speed toward her car. Sorry. He said, sorry, his face continued to stay red the rest of the day. She graciously accepted his apology. The other fella? No show. They would all tell the story from a different point of view. Where would the truth finally lie?

20

ASTRA FISIC AND BROWN'S FOOD TRUCK FLEET

Astra Fisic's friend Franklin Rowdy Benjamin Brown (usually called Brown or FRB) has a meals-on-wheels. The wheels are old, repurposed black hearse. Since he delivers primarily to old folks, shut-ins, and the like he must have a very cheerful attitude because when they see the hearse coming, well…he calls her *Blondie.* Blondie and I will be over soon he tells Mr. Holler, Ms. Peeks, and old(er) Grandma Herring. We'll be right there. Then off he goes with their lunches packaged in nice white paper boxes (not Styrofoam or plastic). He is well known in the community. Astra and Brown have known one another for over thirty years. They met at the County jail where he was detained for protesting about voting rights away back then. Astra was visiting another protester, her second Cousin Reena. Brown and Blondie pulled up to The Café for lunch one Tuesday with Astra. He was wearing his classic bib overalls and a clean but old-looking T-shirt with the faded but readable words, *Prosper Peace*. He still had his DM boots on and his hat was sweaty. She had just removed her red hat and was sliding into a booth. Brown was an organic gardener and had a couple of acres on the edge of town. All the veg he put into the lunches were homegrown and prepared by him or his nephew, Lincoln who often drove Blondie. He was twenty-one and considering finishing college, but not sure where not sure what about. He only needed a semester or two. Seemed a waste not to complete. Even his debt was low. The summer was on them, and they needed to make a few bucks. Who knows what might evolve? He and Astra had dreamed up Blondie, who knows what next?

Astra was having the *BestBurger*, fries (no salt), and salad. Brown liked the look of the *red-white-and-blue* plate, full of chops, greens, sweet po, and a cornbread roll. The last time they got together was for the *Sweet Potato Feastival*, when Astra won that trip up north. Brown had sold her the very potatoes she used for the final winning presentation. He knew Frederick Mason-Dixon well as he was related to his cousin's cousin. Kin. You know. Anyway, the lunches arrived, and they tucked in.

Brown explained how he and Lincoln had widened their scope and the deliveries had almost doubled. There were more needy folks than one might notice, and he thought if he could find another suitable vehicle, they might just buy it and fix it up. Astra told him she knew of an ice cream van that needed some re-purposing but might just help his cause. It was over at the gas station on Hwy 12 near the Manner's Pond. Brown knew the place and texted Lincoln to meet him there in an hour. Might just do the trick!

Astra headed home after a delightful lunch with Brown and Dog was happy to see her. They reclined for half an hour and then went over to see Melodious, who was happily listening to the blues on her headset as she washed the dishes. Astra was always afraid if she just tapped Mel on the shoulder, she'd freak out…but she could not hear, bell, knock, or walk-in. Astra had learned to circle and get seen first then call her name, and if all failed, drop something to get her attention! Whadda hoot. Anyway, Mel was glad to see her, and they sat down for some sweet T. It was hot out there. High 90's and muggy with tornado winds on the horizon. Likely will pass but one never knows. Mel was looking for something new to do with her time. She was newly energized from clearing up her Vit D deficiency. One thing Mel had not talked about much was how much she loved to cook, especially from different countries and cultures. Astra was fascinated.

Brown phoned Astra and reported he and Lincoln had purchased the ice cream -van-soon-to-be-meals-on-wheels-#two and was thrilled. They would have it running like a dream sooner rather than later. Lincoln wanted that to be 'his' and they agreed. Astra tried out something else on him and he thought it brilliant. He would keep his eyes open. They might just find one.

About two weeks later the quilting conference in Kentucky finished and Sarahfinna, ChaChalita, and Roz would be home soon. Astra loved the design those girls did. Why who would have ever thought up their creative ways of putting things together? Not just fabric, there were yarns and ribbons stitched down and 3D pictures of g-kids. Amazing. They always brought her a catalog of the final show and she looked forward to it! Astra had been working on one quilt for nearly three years. Really? Yes. She stitched it all by hand and as she was not that dexterous, she took her time. The colors popped and it would end up a wall hanging in her office over the place where Dog slept.

The phone rang about 10pm. Late for Astra who tucked in early. Was a couple from California (two hours difference in time zones) who had a food truck for sale and seemed to meet the requirements Astra had posted. It would be Brown's third truck, but the cook would be...you guessed it? Melodious! The price was right, and there was truly little fixing-up needed...except painting the outside with Brown's logo and phone number. Other than that, it was ready to go. Now the Powells from Fresno was willing to drive it to Mississippi if Brown & Co. would pay the gas and any servicing needed on the trip. Then they would require a ride down to Jackson to the airport and would fly home. Done. Deal. Astra would have Brown phone the next day. 11amCT.

Melodious was so excited she could hardly sleep. The next day the Powell's would be arriving, and she would join the Brown Fleet. They had named the ice-cream-van *ChocolateCheezecake*, and the new food truck was to be *Red,* just like Melodious' newly dyed hair!

A month later the Fleet was functioning better than Brown, Lincoln, or Melodious could have imagined. Mel cooked whatever Brown wanted for their two trucks (along with Brown's veg). The poor and shut-in got the best and kept track of various comments so they knew what was liked, and well, what could be left off the menu (like okra stew or fried squirrel). Then she cooked for the food truck that had three stops a day at three locations. That is where they made their money to keep all three going. Brilliant. *Blondie, ChocolateCheezecake, and Red* were serviced by Alamo who worked at the truck stop near the highway. He was a genius and if anything was needed, he was their man! Astra looked forward to Mel's variety and at least once a week got lunch from the food truck, took it home, and enjoyed the talents of her friends.

21

ASTRA FISIC AND THE MISSISSIPPI SECRET HOLDERS

Astra Fisic our red-hat-wearing-slightly-retired-astronomer friend uncovered something unpleasant as she looked over Donovan's essay. It was about his desire to become a *secret holder*. Donovan is sixteen. He will be a senior next year. He plays cornhole, runs track, and sometimes wrestles. His Scout program taught the use of weapons (safely of course) and Donovan has a tiny (very tiny) swastika tattooed on his ring finger, under his class ring. Donovan is white, 6'1", big beautiful blue eyes with a greenish tint, a buzz-cut for totally blonde white hair (a toe-head) on top, and a tiny mustache trying to sprout. An average student Donovan has no intention of going to college (community or otherwise) as stated in his essay. He might try the Army or Marines. Why he brought his essay to Astra might be a bit of a mystery so here is the answer: he wanted to.

Donovan had known Astra since he was born as his grandmother, Donut (of the quilt club) and she are great friends. Donut is practically raising Donovan as his parents had issues and his father had gone to prison for four years. When his father came home Donovan was nine, and he noticed all the tats his dad had and when he was eleven, he got that tiny one on his finger, hoping it would make away with his dad. Seems his dad never noticed, and Donovan never knew what the symbol meant until he was much older. Depending upon who he was with he either made sure he had his class ring firmly over it or exposed it by changing the ring to another finger. To date, he did not know what he did not know. That was dangerous.

Astra at Thee Café was having a *red-yellow-and-green plate*…fish tacos with Pico de Gallo, beans, rice, a squirt of guacamole, and flan. She drank a diet 'dew and tried to relax. How do we help one another learn that ideas have consequences? One of her most favorite themes. Percy and Alcor came bopping in and joined her, burgers, and a pita sandwich with guacamole for them. What did they know about the *Secret Holders*? Nothing. What did they know about militias or groups like this in general? Nothing. Would they do some research? Yes. Astra did not need to remind them how untechy she was, so they set off to laptops and computers in the office to search for such a group. The only time Astra had heard about them was when they reported to the 'Capitol insurrection' on January 6, 2021, in Washington DC to 'do their part'. Three of their members were arrested and eventually bailed out by donations from Mississippi members. They still must go to trial.

Donut and Donovan joined Astra Saturday afternoon for late-lunch/early dinner at Thee Café. They had a great visit. Donut was still a bit flabby, especially around the middle, but had been taking better care of herself, under less stress. Her son, they call him Dip Stick, (Donovan's father) was on a rehab program for alcohol and had another (at least) ninety days to go. So, it was just the two of them and peace was usual in the household. It was his essay that had troubled her though and Astra asked if Donut had read it. No. Do you mind if we go over it? Donovan said no. He had no idea how little he knew. In the process she got Donovan to explain who the *secret holders* were and what they believed in, what they did (especially considering Jan 6). His face lit up when he talked about America and what freedom was. He wanted to be an adult member as soon as possible so he might exercise his rights. The leadership of their local was a fella who'd been in the Marines, a Warrant Officer, who knew the ropes. Astra and Donut looked at one another with questions flooding their faces. Why would you want to belong to such a group that hates other groups of people? They began. There is nothing wrong with disagreement, which makes for a wholesome democracy. And over an hour later they had a few answers, and Donovan had many new questions.

It was to become an uncomfortable time for Donut and Donovan now that this was out in the open in their home. She did not want him associating with the youth holders and she certainly did not want him discussing the Marines with the Warrant Officer. Donovan saw it not only as teen-age-angst but as suppression of his 'rights as an American' of freedom of association. Donut figured as he was still sixteen and, in her house, he might abide by her rules, not theirs? He disagreed. He never stopped her from going to quilting club, church, or her Rotary do-gooders. They do not incite riots or kill people as happened on Jan. 6. do they? No. Donovan had to agree.

So, Donovan took another risky path and did two things that backfired. He tried to contact his dad at rehab. Not possible as Dip Stick did not want to talk to him, felt no bond with him, had no responsibility for him. And Donovan went to the internet for his *secret holder's* information. There he could get clear ideas about their practices and ideas. What he got was propaganda. He did not understand the consequences of the *work of the secret holders*. As best he could figure the holders were like the Neo-Confederates that met up near the Tennessee border. Did not like the new Mississippi flag, wanted the battle flag of good-old-Dixie to fly high. They had some neo-Nazi leanings and Donovan was attracted by the notion that white people were superior in every way and therefore should lead. If he had taken even five minutes to consider that his cornhole partner, Raven, a Choctaw and as bright as a morning star, he would have seen the cracks in the theories. He did not.

He did not think. He did not consider. Donovan just boiled with anger and the beginnings of resentful hatred. A psych might say it had a lot to do with his dad…do not know.

Donut stays connected with Astra and tries to keep her head clear enough to respect Donovan's beliefs and still restrict his behavior based on false theories and lies. Mostly she hated the violence and the change in Donovan. He was determined so he joined the Marines and is currently at Basic now that he is eighteen. Who knows what he will learn there, who he will meet and what choices he might change or continue to make? All Astra and Donut want him, and us all to realize, is that ideas have consequences. *Let's storm the Capitol, hang the Vice President, hurt some people, support our President, and stop the peaceful transfer of power* was once only a discussion over a couple of cups of coffee. See where it went? Who knew?

THAT'S ALL Y'ALL.

CPSIA information can be obtained
at www.ICGtesting.com
Printed in the USA
LVHW111225090422
715559LV00001B/30

9 781956 998238